Norse Mythology

Captivating Stories & Timeless Tales of Norse Folklore. The Myths, Sagas & Legends of the Gods, Immortals, Magical Creatures, Vikings & More

History Brought Alive

of any kind are declared or implied. Readers acknowledge that the author is not engaged in the rendering of legal, financial, medical or professional advice. The content within this book has been derived from various sources. Please consult a licensed professional before attempting any techniques outlined in this book.

By reading this document, the reader agrees that under no circumstances is the author responsible for any losses, direct or indirect, that are incurred as a result of the use of the information contained within this document, including, but not limited to, errors, omissions, or inaccuracies.

Greetings!

As fellow passionate readers of history and mythology we aim to create the very best books for our readers.

We invite you to join our VIP list so that you can be the first to receive new books and exclusives. Plus you will receive a free gift!

Sign Up Today

https://www.subscribepage.com/hba

Table of Contents

Introduction

Norse mythology is a truly fascinating ancient mythology filled with epic myths, battles, stories, folklore, gods, goddesses, customs, traditions, and beliefs. Norse mythology can be quite a daunting feat to sink your teeth into due to the immense size and lore associated with the mythology; however, that is where *History Brought Alive* comes in. We want to help you truly appreciate the marvels and wonders of Norse mythology by providing you with all you need to know in one single read. At *History Brought Alive,* we are history and mythology enthusiasts and are inherently fascinated with all the secrets these ancient beliefs, customs, traditions, and myths hold. Join us on a discovery to uncover the path of Norse paganism and learn from the ancient beliefs and customs from one of the most interesting civilizations the world has ever known—the Vikings.

Within these pages, we will not simply rehash the ancient myths, but rather provide context, background, and discussion regarding what life was like during the Viking Age, how life during that era influenced these myths, and how the myths influenced the Vikings. Upon reading, we will help you peel back the complex layers of history that surround these fascinating stories to take a peek at the accurate accounts of the myths, beliefs, customs, and traditions as they actually were.

We will uncover the geography of Norse mythology by understanding how the Vikings viewed the world. The nine realms of Norse mythology included Niflheim, Muspelheim, Asgard, Midgard, Jotunheim, Vanaheim, Svartalfheim, and Helheim. The realms played an integral role in providing explanations to the Vikings about how the world worked, how the gods operated, and how Earth coexisted in the cosmos. The nine realms were not only used to map out the cosmos, but were also used as a means to make sense of the phenomena the Vikings were experiencing.

The creation of the world in terms of Norse mythology will be unpacked, and we will take note of how the world was formed through fire and ice; the story of how the realms were created and the unusual origin of the gods, giants, and mortals; how the gods reigned supreme, and how the dynamic of the cosmos came to fruition. The creation myth is highly significant, as it provides the much-needed context of the history of the cosmos and the nine realms that coexist within it.

We will unpack what the customs, traditions, and worship looked like during the Viking age. How did the Vikings live their lives? How did they worship the gods? What did a day in the life of a Viking look like? Understanding how the Vikings worshipped the gods and what traditions they practiced provides us with a sneak peek back to the age of the Vikings to see how the myths influenced their daily lives.

Next, we will introduce the Norse gods in all their glory and signify what they stood for and their sphere of influence over Nordic culture. What they represented, who they were, and the myths surrounding their legacy will all be discussed. Understanding the gods and goddesses is vital, as they are the key characters that will be present in the myths of this fascinating mythology. Gods and goddesses such as Odin, Frigg, Baldur, Thor, Heimdallr, Loki, and more will be discussed and analyzed in detail throughout these pages. We need to understand the gods and their power to truly understand the essence of Norse mythology, as without the gods, there are no myths.

While it is important to uncover the myths, it is as important to highlight where the myths come from. The myths come from two crucial sources of evidence, which together is practically all we know about Norse mythology to date. The sources from which practically every story, myth, or folklore comes from are either thanks to the Poetic Edda or Prose Edda. We will uncover the epic poems of the Edda, as within these poems lies all the secrets and knowledge we know about the Norse gods. Without the poems from the Eddas, we would largely be left in the dark regarding the ancient beliefs of the Vikings, and thus, it is critical to uncover the poems that lie within these ancient scripts. Over and above, the poems from Eddas' many other myths will be uncovered and discussed. The ancient stories of Norse mythology will slowly begin to unravel, and we will marvel at the fascinating adventures and tales the Nordic people had to tell. One myth, in particular, is truly frightening, and that is the myth of Ragnarok. This is the myth that ends all myths. It is the equivalent of the apocalypse, and signifies the destruction of all that we know and everything in the cosmos, including the Norse gods.

However, it is not just us that are fascinated with Norse mythology. Norse mythology has had a modern resurgence in the public consciousness through various depictions and portrayals of the Norse myths and gods through pop culture. Norse mythology's influence over Marvel's comic line *Thor*, the *Lord of the Rings*, *Game of Thrones*, *God of War*, and many more has truly relit the torch of ancient mythology.

The legends, myths, and stories are all here just waiting to be read. Everything you need to know about the Vikings and the Norse pantheon is neatly wrapped up in one single read; all you need to do is uncover the secrets of Nordic history. Discover what life was like as a Viking and what governed their customs, traditions, and beliefs.

Chapter 1: The Geography and Realms of Norse Mythology

Norse mythology originated in the Scandinavian region located in Northern Europe. This region is categorized by the Scandanavian peninsula. There are five countries that make up this region, which include Norway, Denmark, Sweden, Finland, and Iceland. Scandinavia was home to the Vikings (a collective term for all people who lived in the Scandinavian region), or more correctly known as Norsemen.

Due to the Vikings living right on the cuff of the Scandinavian sea, they would often go on voyages to different lands and pillage there. They were infamous in England, as the Vikings would often set voyage there and raid nearby villages. Vikings were seen as heathens and pagans by the English. Due to the excessive and violent raids on England, the Vikings became public enemy number one to them, and the fact that they were pagans and heathens only enraged the English even more. However, England was not the only target on the Vikings' radar; they would raid and voyage all over Europe, and during the period of 800AD and 1100AD, they left a crucial fingerprint on the history of Europe. However, although the Vikings were leaving a mark in Europe at the time, that was only one of nine realms that the Norsemen believed in. The Norsemen followed the teachings and traditions of Norse mythology as a guiding light for their actions.

The Nine Realms

Within Norse mythology, there are said to be nine realms within the universe. These made up the cosmos and were interconnected with one another. These included Niflheim, Muspelheim, Asgard, Midgard, Jotunheim, Vanaheim, Alfheim, Svartalfheim, and Helheim (Skjalden, 2011). Each realm has specific purposes and features that distinctly separate them from one another. Each one of these nine realms was home to various kinds of beings and mythical creatures. Jotumheim was home to the giants, Asgard was home to the gods, and Midgard was home to the humans. Norsemen believed that the nine different realms were held together by the world tree of Yggdrasil. Yggdrasil was the instrument that would ensure each realm was connected within a larger universe (Skjalden, 2011).

The first two realms include Niflheim and Muspelheim. These two are believed to have been created out of Ginnungagap. Ginnungagap consists of two words being merged together; the words in question were ginnunga and gap. Gap can be directly translated, as it is in English, but the word ginnunga is more difficult to translate. According to the Dutch scholar of Germanic linguistics and Germanic mythology, the word 'ginnunga' can be understood as something that is 'magically-charged' (Skjalden, 2020). Thus, Ginnungagap is known as the yawning void of absolute emptiness with a magically charged center that led to the creation of the first two realms. The cosmos had not been created yet, as all that had been created was Niflheim in the north and Muspelheim in the south.

However, the other seven realms were birthed out of Ymir's body (a hermaphroditic giant and one of the first-ever giants to ever exist in Norse mythology), which was initiated by Odin and his brothers during the creation of the cosmos (Skjalden, 2020). The fact that there are nine realms is no coincidence. The number nine holds great significance, much of which can be found in various poems, such as in the Eddas by Snorri Sturluson. Just to mention a few occurrences of the significance of the number can be found when Odin was hung on Yggdrasil for nine days and nights, Heimdallr birthed nine daughters, and Njord (the god of the wind and the sea) waited nine days for his wife Skadi (Skjalden, 2011).

Niflheim

Niflheim can be described as the realm of fog and mist. Niflheim, also known as *Niðavellir* in Old Norse, can be translated to 'mist home' or 'mist world.' Niflheim is located in the Northern region of Ginnungagap and is the first realm and was created at the same time as Muspelheim. Niflheim is the darkest and coldest realm of all the worlds. Hvergelmir is the oldest spring in all of Norse mythology, and is located in Niflheim. It is believed Hvergelmir is protected by an enormous and ferocious dragon known as Nidhug, or *Níðhöggr* in Old Norse (Skjalden, 2011).

According to Norse mythology experts, it is said that freezing cold rivers branch off of Hvergelmir and are believed to be the primary source of the eleven rivers (*Élivágar*) of Niflheim. These eleven rivers were the first rivers the universe had ever known as they were the only rivers in the only realm that existed at the time that had water. Hvergelmir is incredibly significant, as it was the primary source of all that is living, as well as the spring that all living beings will return to one day. It is said that the freezing water that flowed from Élivágar down the vast mountain ranges of Ginnungagap gradually solidified into a large dense layer of frost and ice, forming new land. Yggdrasil, the world tree, began to grow, stretched one of its three roots into the spring of Hvergelmir, and drew the necessary water needed to branch out (Skjalden, 2011).

Muspelheim

Muspelheim, or *Múspellsheimr* in Old Norse, can be described as the realm of fire. This realm was created at the same time as Niflheim; however, it is located in the South of

Ginnungagap. Muspelheim is the polar opposite of Niflheim. Niflheim is the coldest realm while Muspelheim is the hottest. According to Norse mythology experts, Muspelheim is a scorching hot world that is filled with erupting volcanoes, lava rivers, flames, sparks, and heavy soot (Skjalden, 2011). It is believed that the sun, the moon, and the stars were created from the sparks of Muspelheim.

According to some traditions, it was believed that the warm air from Muspelheim resulted in the ice of Niflheim melting, thus creating the form of Ymir, the father of the evil giants and the first known being to inhabit the world. Ymir would be killed by Odin and other gods. His death would result in the creation of the other realms, as Odin and his brothers created the rest of the worlds with the corpse of Ymir. Ymir's death would also be the catalyst of Ragnarök and the end of the world by fire. Thus, Ymir was both responsible for the creation and destruction of the world (Britannica, 2019).

Muspelheim is home to the fire giants and the fire demons and is ruled by the great fire giant Surtr. Surtr is a sworn enemy of the Aesir (the inhabitants of Asgard such as Odin, Thor, Heimdallr, Loki) and has declared war on them for the death of his father Ymir. He would one day lead the sons of Muspelheim to destroy the world by fire during Ragnarök (Britannica, 2019). Ragnarök will be discussed in greater detail in a later chapter.

Asgard

Asgard, or *Ásgarðr* in Old Norse, is the third realm and is located in the middle of the world high up in the sky, which is unapproachable to mortal men. Asgard is the home of the gods, the goddesses, and the Aesir tribe. It is home to well-known gods such as Odin, Thor, Heimdallr, Loki, Frigg, Idun, Bragi, Tyr, and many more. The ruler of Asgard is Odin. He is known as the All-Father, and he is the chief ruler of the Aesir tribe. Odin's wife is Frigg, and she is the queen of all of Asgard (Skjalden, 2011). Many scholars believe that Asgard was a magnificent celestial city full of palaces made out of gold and silver, which was built entirely by the Aesir.

Asgard in itself is further divided into 12 smaller realms. The most significant of these realms include Valhalla and Fólkvangr. Inside these gates are inhabited by the gods alongside Viking warriors who died in battle. The fallen warriors are divided equally regarding where they spend the rest of eternity post mortem. Half of these warriors would end up in Valhalla, which is ruled by Odin, and the other half of the warriors would end up in Fólkvangr, which is ruled by the goddess Freya (Skjalden, 2011).

Asgard is protected by a giant wall that surrounds the entire realm. The wall was built during the battle against the Vanir (the other tribe of gods who were sworn enemies of the Aesir). If it were not for the wall, the Aesir and Asgard would be defenseless. This wall was impenetrable and was incredibly strong, which offered the Aesir complete protection against their enemies such as the evil giants, fire demons, the Vanir, and many more. There was only one entry within the wall that would lead into Asgard, and it was known as the Great Gate.

Within Asgard, there is a bridge that connects Asgard to all the other realms, including Midgard (the home of mortals). This bridge is known as Bifrost, but it has also been known to be called the rainbow bridge. Bifrost is described as a rainbow that consists of three plaited strands of fire. Bifrost was expertly guarded by the Norse god Heimdallr, who made sure that no trespassers or ambushes would fall upon Agard. Heimdallr had extraordinary powers and possessed remarkable sight that would help him spot enemies from a mile away. Whenever Bifrost was in danger, Heimdallr would blow his trumpet, the Gjallarhorn, and warn the gods of any danger ahead (Ancient Pages, 2016).

Midgard

Midgard, also known as *Miðgarðr* in Old Norse, is the fourth realm, and can be translated as "middle earth." Midgard is the realm that is home to human beings and animals. Midgard is located in the center of the world right below Asgard, which floats above Midgard. According to legend, Midgard was created from the body of Ymir. When Odin and his brothers killed Ymir, they are said to have rolled the evil giant's body into the central void of the universe, which began the formation and geographical creation of Midgard. Ymir's flesh is said to be the land of Midgard. The oceans are the blood of Ymir; his bones became the mountains; his teeth became the cliffs; his hair became the trees, and Ymir's scattered brain became the clouds. It is said that four dwarves, known as Nordi, Surdi, Austri, and Vestri, who represent the four points of the compass, held up Ymir's skull, and thus, his skull became the dome of the heavens. The moon, the stars, and the sun, as we know them, were created from the scattered sparks that were caught within the skull of Ymir (Britannica, 2019a).

The first-ever humans in Norse mythology are believed to be Ask and Embla, who were sent down to Midgard after they were created from tree logs by Odin and his brothers (Skjalden, 2011). Midgard and Asgard are connected by Bifrost, which is guarded by Heimdallr. Scholars believed that Midgard was surrounded by an enormous ocean that was impassable by mere mortals.

It is believed that this impassable ocean was occupied by a ferocious sea serpent, known as the Midgard Serpent, which would devour any person who dared try to cross the ocean. The serpent was so large that it was believed it could encircle the realm of Midgard in its entirety with ease.

Jotunheim

Jotunheim, also known as *Jötunheimr,* is the fifth realm, and is home to the giants, or *jötnar,* as they are called in Old Norse. Jotunheim is only separated from Asgard due to the river Iving, which is believed to ever freeze over, thus acting as a barrier between the two realms. The giants are yet another sworn enemy of the Aesir and strive for the downfall of the gods. The geography of Jotunheim mainly consists of vast dense forests, rocky landscapes, and wilderness. Jotunheim is also said to be very cold and lies on the snowy region of the outermost shores of the ocean, thus is inhabited by many frost giants (Skjalden, 2011).

Due to this, the giants would eat fish from the rivers and oceans, as well as the animals from the forest, as it is believed that there was no fertile land in Jotunheim to grow crops or vegetables. The Aesir and the giants are said to have been constantly waged in the battle against one another; however, interestingly enough, it was said that their love affairs between the two races would sometimes occur and mixed-race offspring were conceived. It is said that even gods such as Thor, Loki, and even Odin himself, had lovers who were giants. Loki, the god of mischief, was actually born in Jotunheim, and was the adopted son of Odin. Loki was accepted with open arms by the Aesir and lived peacefully in Asgard for many years until he was punished and exiled and sent back to live in Jotunheim.

Utgard is the stronghold that protects Jotunheim, and can be described as the giants' version of Asgard's great wall. Utgard is said to be so tall that it is almost impossible to see the top of it. Utgard is a fortress that has been formed as a result of carved blocks of snow and sharp glistening icicles. Inside this fortress lives the much-feared giant ruler, king Utgard-Loki (Skjalden, 2011).

Vanaheim

Vanaheim, also known as *Vanaheimr* in Old Norse, is the sixth realm in Norse mythology and is home to the Vanir gods. The Vanir gods were associated with health, fertility, and wisdom. The Vanir gods are an old branch of gods who have had a conflict with the Aesir throughout their history. The Vanir gods and Aesir gods once lived in Asgard as one; however, conflict broke loose and the two branches of gods battled it out to fight for who got to live in Asgard. The bloody warfare eventually came to an end and the Aesir came out victorious. As a result, almost all of the Vanir gods were banished from Asgard; however, some Vanir gods still lived in Asgard after the war. At the end of the Aesir-Vanir war, three of the main gods of the Vanir clan stayed in Asgard as a token of peace. The Vanir gods in question were Njord, Freyr, and Freya (Skjalden, 2011).

Much of the geography of Vanaheim is a mystery. Many scholars have struggled to find any reputable sources or documentation about the realm of Vanaheim. It is known the Vanaheim is a place of magic and sorcery, as the Vanir gods were masters of the magic arts and were also believed to have been able to predict the future. However, nobody actually knows where the land of Vanaheim is located, nor are there any accounts of what it looks like.

Alfheim

Alfheim is the seventh realm in Norse mythology and is also known as *Álfheimr,* or *Ljósálfheimr* in Old Norse. It is located right next to Asgard in the heavens. Alfheim is home to the light elves, who are described as the most beautiful creatures known to man; they have even been described as being more beautiful than the sun itself. Not much is known about the home of the Alfheim, but considering its inhabitants being the light elves, it is considered by scholars to be a world of grace, light, and overwhelming beauty.

The light elves are widely considered to be guardian angels of Norse mythology. The Vanir god Freyr is the ruler of Alfheim. The light elves are considered gods in themselves; however, they are believed to be minor gods. They are gods of nature and fertility, and they help assist or even hinder humans with their knowledge of magical powers. The light elves often appear in art, such as paintings and music, and are believed to be the inspiration for many artists during the Viking Age (Norse Mythology for Smart People, 2018).

Svartalfheim

Svartalfheim is the eighth realm in Norse mythology, and is also known as *Niðavellir* or *Svartálfaheimr;* the word Svartalfheim can be translated to 'dark fields.' Thus, the realm was dark and consisted of many dense forests and caves that spread across the realm, almost like a whimsical, magical forest.

Svartalfheim is home to the dwarves. The dwarves of Svartalfheim are believed to have lived under rocks, in caves, or have found shelter underground. The dwarves were believed to be incredibly talented craftsmen and had gifted the gods of Asgard many powerful gifts such as the magical ring Draupnir and Odin's spear, Gungnir (Skjalden, 2011).

The king of the dwarves was Hreidmar, and was the ruler of the realm right up until he was killed by Fáfnir. Heirdmar had a lavish house built out of glittering gold and flashing gems and was guarded by none other than Fáfnir himself. Fáfnir grew ill-natured, killed Heirdmar, and stole all of Heirdmar's gold. He then ventured into the deep forests, where it is believed that Fáfnir turned into a serpent or a dragon (it varies in different sources) in order to guard his stolen treasure against thieves (Wikipedia, 2021).

Helheim

Helheim is the ninth and final realm, and is home to the dishonorable dead. Helheim can be understood as the Norse hell. In Norse mythology, Helheim is often simply referred to as Hel. This is where all the souls of the wicked and dishonest end up after death, such as thieves, murderers, cowards, and anybody who the gods and goddesses feel are not worthy or brave enough to enter Valhalla or Folkvangr.

Helheim is ruled by Hel, who is the daughter of Loki. Unlike hell, as we know it from a Christian perspective, where hell is described as scorching hot, Helheim is the complete contrast. It is believed to be freezing cold. Helheim is described as a dark, grim, and freezing realm where nobody will ever feel joy or happiness for the rest of eternity. Hel is believed to use all the dead in Helheim as her own personal army at her disposal to attack the gods and goddesses during Ragnarök and unleash her troop of the undead at the plains of Vigrid. When this happens, it is believed to be the end of the world. (Skjalden, 2011).

Chapter 2: Norse Mythology Origins

Every culture, religion, and region has its own interpretation of how the universe came into fruition and how the gods were created. Norse mythology is no different. Norse mythology has its own interpretation of the creation of the universe, and is used to explain the workings of the universe. It was used to explain aspects of life that mankind was unable to explain at the time, and the unknown phenomenon that the Vikings experienced in their everyday lives was often attributed to deities, monsters, and fate.

Throughout history, one of the biggest questions on everybody's minds has always been how the world and mankind was created. Before the breakthrough of scientific discoveries in the 20th century, there were absolutely no explanations for the creation of the universe and everything in it other than the supernatural. Thus, the Norsemen, like every other ancient culture before them, had their own explanation as to how the world came into fruition, and it involved supernatural and otherworldly powers wrapped in myths and epic tales.

Many of the aspects regarding the creation of the universe from a Norse mythological perspective seem familiar and are shared to an extent among other mythological beliefs. However, some of the myths and aspects of the Norse creation myth are especially fantastical and surprising.

The Creation of the Universe, the Gods, and Man

According to Norse mythology, the cosmos began with an empty void of magical power known as Ginnungagap (as mentioned in Chapter 1). In the north of Ginnungagap, there was a well-known Hvergelmir, which was the sole water source of the universe and streamed directly into the great world tree, Yggdrasil. The northern region of Ginnungagap was extremely cold and was known as the coldest region of the universe. While the water from Hvergelmir flowed into Yggdrasil, there was an excess amount of water that was not being absorbed by the world tree. Thus, the water that was not being absorbed by Yggdrasil quickly froze, and gradually grew en masse. This mass of frozen wasteland created a world of ice and frost, which formed the world of Niflheim (Greenberg, 2020).

However, at the same time, the southern region of Ginnungagap was extremely hot, and as time went on, the southern region grew hotter and hotter by the day. The heat led to a landmass of lava, flames, and fire, and the world known as Muspelheim was formed. The intense heat that radiated from Muspelheim rose and made its way to the frosty land of Niflheim. The heat from Muspelheim caused the ice to melt from Niflheim, and water droplets from the ice began to drip down to the land below. When the water droplets from the ice voyaged all the way from Niflheim to Muspelheim, the drops caused sparks to shoot up from below (Greenberg, 2020).

When the extreme cold and extreme heat from Niflheim and Muspelheim mixed and collided with one another, the start of life was birthed. The water droplets from Niflheim began to melt and drop down to the fiery depths of

Muspelheim; a phenomenon occurred within Ginnungagap. As the two climates mixed with one another, steam began to be produced and rose. The mists formed and began to swirl in Ginnungagap until it was concentrated. Humanoid form took shape. With everything working in synergy, the steam, the heat from Muspelheim, and the melted ice droplets from Niflheim, the birth of Ymir commenced, and the first living creature and giant was born.

However, Ymir was not the only giant that was birthed from this phenomenon. Another giant by the name of Auðumla was also created. Auðumla was a giant primordial cow. Although Ymir was born first, he was trapped in an icy prison deep in the walls of the ice of Niflheim. Centuries passed, and Ymir remained trapped.

Over the years, Auðumla would lick the frost off of t Ymir's skin, eventually freeing the giant from his icy prison. According to the myth of creation, Ymir would feed on Auðumla's milk, and Auðumla would feed off the salt that had gathered on the icy rocks of Niflheim. For centuries, all that was in existence in the universe was Ginnungagap, Niflheim, Muspelheim, Ymir, and Auðumla. Many years passed, and Ymir and Auðumla would live together peacefully. However, that would change as time went on, and as Ymir fed off the milk of Auðumla, Auðumla fed off the ice of Niflheim. As the cow would do this, a large dent of Niflheim would be lost. Where Auðumla licked, the ice would take shape, and eventually, the land formed the shape of Búri, the first god of the known universe (Greenberg, 2020).

Búri was born, and because of this, so was the bloodline of the gods. Búri would go on to have at least one more child; however, even amongst experts, it is unknown how Búri conceived the child or how the child was born. Regardless, Búri had a son, and his name was Borr. The accounts differ, but it is said that Búri had another child, a daughter named Bestla, who was the first-ever goddess. Borr would go on to marry Bestla. However, other accounts say that Bestla was formed from the sweat of Ymir and was the first frost jotunn (giant).

Just as Búri had children, so did Ymir. It is said while Ymir slept, he would perspire from the heat that radiated from Muspelheim; two beads of sweat fell from his arm, creating one male and female jotunn, and from his legs, he produced a six-headed son (Geller, 2016). Ymir's male and female offspring would procreate, resulting in the next generation of frost jötnar. Ymir also sweated out his son, Surt, who was an evil flaming giant who traveled down to Muspelheim, whose fire made Surt feel welcome (New World Encyclopedia, 2020). Surt would go on to become the ruler of Muspelheim and the other fire giants that would be born in later generations (Greenberg, 2020).

However, whether Bestla was a daughter of Ymir or the daughter of Búri will always be a debate amongst experts in mythology. Although, what is not a debate and is agreed upon by the university is that Búri's son, Borr, married Bestla, and they had three sons. The three sons that Bestla gave birth to were considered gods, and they were named Odin, Vili, and Vé.

Centuries passed, and Ymir had now become the father to and ruled an army of frost giants. Ymir and his army were considered incredibly cruel and evil, and as a result, the three sons of Bestla and Borr planned to eliminate Ymir and all those that followed him, as he was perceived as a great threat to the cosmos.

Odin and his two brothers carried out their hunt and successfully slew Ymir. Many experts debate that the reason Odin and his brothers slew Ymir was so that they could use his bodily remains to create other worlds; others debate that they killed Ymir because he was an evil entity in the universe. However, the motives behind Odin and his brothers' crusade will remain a mystery and be a topic of debate for eternity. However, it is said that when Odin and his brothers killed Ymir, the amount of blood the giant spewed out was so immense that it drowned all the jötnar but two. The only two surviving frost jötnar were Bergelmir and Ymir's wife, whose name is unknown. These surviving frost jötnar would repopulate and wage lifelong warfare and hatred among the Aesir gods (Learn Religions, 2016).

Odin, Vili, and Vé left Ymir's corpse in the center of Ginnungagap and then used the remainder of Ymir's rotting body to create a new world known as Midgard, which would be placed in the center of the Yggdrasil. The brothers made use of Ymir's body to act as the surface of the world and his blood to form the oceans, seas, and rivers. Odin used Ymir's bones and his teeth to make the mountains and fjords.

To make the sky, the brothers placed Ymir's skull over the new world of Midgard and used his brains to create clouds. Every part of Ymir's body created Midgard, and eventually became home to the mortals and animals. Midgard is

Earth as we know it as human beings. Midgard was placed in the central region of Yggdrasiland and is often referred to as Middle Earth, due to its location in the cosmos.

However, Odin and his brothers did not stop there. They went on to capture all of the sparks that shot up from Muspelheim and place them within Midgard's new sky. These sparks brought light to the new world and were used to create the sun, the moon, and the stars.

Ymir's remains were fully utilized, and Midgard was complete; however, Odin and his brothers knew that the jötnar would want revenge for what happened to their ruler and father, thus they recognized that the jötnar would pose a threat to the Aesir and humanity. To counteract this, Ymir's eyebrows were used to form a protective wall that encircled Midgard and kept this new world safe from any attacks initiated from the jötnar (Greenberg, 2020).

Odin, Vili, and Vé were incredibly pleased with the new world they had created, and decided they wanted to bring life to their new world by creating new people and animals to inhabit Midgard. Odin and his brothers went on to create the first man and woman; they were known as Ask and Embla. They were given life by the brothers as a result of being carved out of the branches of trees in Midgard.

Odin and his brothers went on to create six new realms, bringing the total number of realms in the universe to nine. Odin, Vili, and Vé settled in Asgard, and the realm of the Aesir gods came into existence.

As the myths progressed, and over time, Vili and Vé became absent and were no longer mentioned; however, Odin went on to become the chief and ruler of the Aesir. Odin married Frigg, the goddess of fertility, marriage, and family. Odin became the All-Father of the Norse world and the most powerful god of them all (Greenberg, 2020).

Chapter 3: Norse Traditions, Worship, and Sacrifice

The Vikings of Scandinavia at the time were pagans. This ultimately means that Vikings practiced polytheism, and thus worshiped multiple gods as opposed to one god, such as how it is done in Christianity. Within Norse mythology, there are numerous gods and goddesses; however, unlike other ancient civilizations at the time, the Vikings had not organized a conventional priesthood or instilled a hierarchy of religious leaders. The Vikings were, for the most part, an oral civilization, and thus were not a civilization of people who tended to document their history, as most Vikings were largely illiterate. The pagan Vikings also did not build grand temples or religious buildings in honor of their religious views, unlike other beliefs and religions at the time. The lack of documentation and concrete evidence on how the Vikings worshipped their gods is a difficult puzzle to piece together.

Norse Mythology Religious practices and Rituals Practiced by Vikings

Norsemen, or Vikings, are well-known for the exploits in battle, voyages, and raids. However, according to Norse mythology experts, it is believed that the Vikings were also known for adopting religious and ritual practices as an important part of their culture and everyday lives. The Vikings' religious beliefs incorporated the worship of many different gods and goddesses; as a result, it is considered that the Vikings believed in a non-doctrinal community religion. What this means is that the Norsemen's beliefs and rituals varied among different regions of Scandinavia.

Although all the regions of Scandinavia worshipped the same gods and held similar beliefs, there were no exact principles in place or set practices that had to be followed by the book...as there was no book. Vikings worshipped the gods they felt were most relevant to their lives and who they believed would bestow them with good fortune.

Vikings were also believed to have worshipped their ancestors, many of which had fallen in battle. According to experts, Vikings largely partook in attempting to communicate with their ancestors' spirits, practiced in the arts of divination and sorcery. The Vikings also practiced a wide variety of different burial practices. These various rituals would often occur within and between various Viking communities.

Due to the Vikings largely being an oral community and very rarely documented their rituals and practices on paper, the accounts of the Viking era were largely written by outsiders rather than firsthand accounts from the Vikings themselves. What we understand today regarding Viking worship and traditions may not be fully understood with complete accuracy, as they are written based on the accounts of witnesses, hearsay, or written many years after the Viking era had occurred.

Thus, as a result, Norse worship and rituals are often conflicting, relatively inaccurate, or even made up by enemies of the Vikings, such as the British, to paint the Norsemen in a bad light, or sometimes to simply tell a more tantalizing story of the mysterious Vikings. However, according to Norse mythology experts, these seven rituals are generally considered to have been traditionally practiced by the Vikings during the Viking Age. These rituals include the blot sacrifice, human sacrifice, Yule celebration, burial traditions, warding off draugr, wedding ceremonies, infant rituals, and naming rituals (Esser, 2018).

Blot Sacrifice

The blot sacrifice was one of the most highly respected traditions in Viking society. The purpose of the blot sacrifice was to secure the good faith and goodwill of the gods for you and your family. This ritual would be carried out with a large group of people on the estate of the local chief of the region. The chief would act as the 'priest,' or commissioner of the sacrifices during the ceremony. The blot sacrifice was an opportunity not only for the public to honor the gods with sacrifices they felt fitting, but also acted as an opportunity for the chief of the region to show off their wealth to the community.

According to Norse mythology experts, a blot sacrifice would happen four times in a year. It would occur at the close of the winter solstice, spring equinox, summer solstice, and autumn equinox. However, certain years had exceptions, and there would be more than four blot sacrifices if the community was experiencing problems such as a bad harvest. One of the very few detailed descriptions of the blot sacrifice ritual was written by Snorri Sturluson in the 13th Century. The detailed account of the ritual stated that all the local farmers of the region would come forth to the chief's temple and sacrifice many animals. The animals that were sacrificed the most were horses. The chief would use twigs to spray blood across the temple, as well as spray blood on the faces of the farmers who offered sacrifices (Esser, 2018).

It was customary to bring with you your own cooked meat and beer, which would be blessed by the chief of the blot sacrifice. When everybody gathered together after the sacrifices had been made, they would drink beer and toast to Odin, the other gods, and their ancestors.

Human Sacrifice

Human sacrifices were not a common occurrence within Viking life, but they were practiced from time to time. As stated earlier, many stories regarding the Vikings are often fabricated and told in such a way as to portray the Scandinavians in a negative light; however, archaeological remains that have been found from expeditions indicate that, on occasion, the Vikings did occasionally partake in human sacrifice (Esser, 2018).

One source of a secondhand account of human sacrifice in the Viking age was written by Adam of Bremen in the 11th Century. Adam writes about the tradition of human sacrifice that would be practiced at Uppsala, Sweden at the beginning of spring once every nine years. According to the account, the ritual was meant to last nine days, and every day, nine sacrifices were made and a feast was enjoyed. That is a total of 81 sacrifices during the festival's ritual.

On each day, one human male would be sacrificed along with eight male animal sacrifices. It is said that the bodies were hung from trees just outside of the temple in which the ritual had occurred. The purpose of this ritual was to honor the All-Father Odin and secure victory in all of the Vikings' battles in the coming year.

According to experts, it is said that the sacrifices were normally criminals or slaves; however, one year a king was sacrificed at Uppsala as a sign of good faith to Odin to bring an end to the extreme famine that the region was experiencing. According to Snorri Sturluson's saga, it is said that the previous two years before the king was sacrificed, the Vikings sacrificed a group of oxen to bring an end to the famine. When the group of oxen failed the following year, they sacrificed a group of men, but still, the famine persisted. The public blamed the king for their misfortune, and thus sacrificed him to Odin and covered the altar in the king's blood (Esser, 2018).

Yule Celebration

Believe it or not, the Vikings celebrated a festival that has incredible similarities to the Christian holiday of Christmas. There are a lot of differences, but there are some interesting similarities. This is largely due to the fact that many Christmas and Christian traditions were borrowed, or born, out of Pagan traditions and were reframed for a Christian audience in mind.

What is most similar about these two holidays is the tree. The Vikings' Yule celebration implemented a tree that symbolized Yggdrasil (the world tree), and Vikings all over Scandinavia would decorate their houses with trees known as Yule trees this time of year. According to experts, it is believed that the Yule tree actually inspired the Christmas tree that is ever present in millions of family homes across the globe come the 25th of December (Ancient Pages, 2020).

The Yule tree to the Vikings was not only symbolic of the world tree that connects the nine realms together, but it was also a symbolic reminder to the Vikings that even during the dark and cold winters Scandanvia experiences, the sun will return and provide great harvests for the Vikings in the months to follow. To highlight even more similarities between the Christmas tree and the Yule tree is that the Vikings were believed to have decorated the Yule tree with a little statue carved to look like the Norse pantheon. Sounds familiar to Christmas trees being decorated with candy canes, bells, socks, and stars, right? The Vikings were also known to leave out food and clothes by the Yule tree as they attempted to call the spirits of the forest. This is similar to how

Christans leave out milk and cookies for Santa Claus. The spirits of the forest that the Vikings were trying to invite into their homes with food and clothes were known as væittir (väittar in Swedish). These were woodland creatures that were believed to live in trees. However, it was a common belief among Vikings that the small creatures would freeze in the forest due to the harsh icy conditions of winter during the time of the Yule celebration. The Vikings did not want the væittir to meet such a grim end, thus they took the trees inside (which were the Yule trees) so that the væittir could have a home in the Vikings' houses during the treacherous winter. Thus, the Vikings opened their homes to the væittir and provided these spirits a warm and cozy atmosphere. This showed a very different side of the Vikings' general perceived nature. For a civilization of people considered to be savages and ferocious brutes, this was a very human and empathetic emotional side of the Vikings that is too often ignored. It is important to remember that Vikings were humans too and not just blood-thirsty warriors.

The actual celebration of the Yule holiday was celebrated by the Vikings on the winter solstice, which begins on the 21st of December. What's interesting is to note how closely the holidays of

Christmas and the Yule celebration are celebrated on the annual calendar. Yet another similarity between the two holidays. What's more is, while Christians celebrate Christmas in remembrance of Jesus Christ, the Vikings celebrate Yule in honor of Odin and the Norse gods. Funny enough, Odin has many a time been compared to Santa Claus. Perhaps this is due to Odin's elderly appearance and long flowing white beard.

The word Jól in Old Norse can be translated to a feast, and the word Jólablót, which was the traditional name for the Yule festival, means midwinter festival and is associated with the rebirth of the sun. This is because the Yule festival happened on the shortest day of the year. The sun would only be visible for a few hours, and in some parts of Scandinavia, it could barely be seen at all. Thus, the festival was centered around the rebirth of the sun, and that from here on out, the light would be more frequent (Ancient Pages, 2020).

The Yule celebration was a day that was keenly awaited by all Vikings, and was a day marked on every Viking's calendar. It was a special tradition to the Nordic people and was practiced in Iceland, Denmark, Norway, and Sweden. According to scholars and extracts from the famed Icelandic Sagas, the Yule celebration was meant to last three full days and nights. During the Yule celebration, Vikings would get together for a massive feast and would invite their friends, families, neighbors, and whoever else wanted to join in the festivities. It was a time for good company, good food, and worship to the Norse pantheon. Everybody would gather around a long table, known as the Yule table, to eat and engage in lovely conversation. Everybody would bring with them a variety of different foods, from fish, to meat, to beer; you name it, the Yule table had it. It was a time for good wholesome fun.

During the Yule celebration, entertainment was a must and the Norsemen would generally participate in singing, dancing, playing games, and telling captivating stories. It is important to note that during the Yule celebration, everybody was invited to participate, even foreigners and travelers from distant lands. In fact, Vikings actually loved when travelers from other parts of the world would join in the festivities. The Vikings enjoyed hearing stories from these travelers about their foreign lands and voyages. For a Viking, travel was key, and thus, they were always fascinated with the ins and outs of what was happening across the world.

Burial Traditions

During the Viking Age, the dead were generally honored in one of two ways when they were sent to the afterlife. For most Vikings, the dead would be given a ceremony to help guide their souls to the afterlife either in the form of cremation or burial. The ceremony was thought to help guide the souls of the fallen Vikings either to Valhalla (the home of Odin and the Norse version of heaven) or Helheim. However, where the fallen Vikings ended up after their life on Midgard (Earth) would be determined by their actions when they were alive. Those pure of heart would be rewarded by spending the rest of eternity within Valhalla, although it was also believed if a Viking died a warrior's death, they would have a better chance ending up in Valhalla . However, those who had committed horrific acts of injustice or had a corrupted soul would spend the rest of eternity in the depths of Helheim.

Cremation was generally used as a means to honor the dead of early Vikings, as they were fiercely paagan, and the act of cremation was practiced upon a funeral pyre. The reason for being cremated instead of buried was because it was believed that the smoke from the fire that scorched their lifeless bodies would act as a carrier to guide their souls to the gates of Valhalla. Once the deceased Viking's corpse had been devoured by the flames, leaving nothing but ash and bones, the remains would be placed in an urn and the rest would be buried in the ground.

When the Vikings honored the dead, whether it was in relation to burials or cremated remains, the location ranged widely. Locations of the burial generally consisted of shallowly-dug graves and large burial mounds that were dug with the intention of holding multiple corpses. There were also groupings of mounds known as grave fields, which served the purpose of what could now be understood as a cemetery.

These Viking cemeteries were specifically designed to resemble the shape of a ship. This was because ships were regarded as incredibly sacred symbols and were considered to be the apparatus that would guide the fallen Vikings safely to Valhalla, similarly to how the smoke from cremated bodies would guide the souls of the dead to the afterlife. This was done by placing stones, or systematically burning graves in the outline of a vessel's shape

The common Viking could not be buried with their actual boat, as ships were far too valuable, thus against popular belief; boat funerals were extremely rare. However, the grave mounds that were made to symbolize a ship were the alternative for almost every Viking that was buried. Boat funerals, as depicted in media such as *History Channel's* highly esteemed TV series *Vikings* were solely reserved for very highly-ranked warriors and Norsemen. Only a very select few Vikings were granted the honor of being buried with their actual boats (Morgan, 2018). What was even rarer was for Norsemen to be cremated at sea with their ship, which would be set on fire due to a fiery arrow being shot from the shores from the hand of an archer. What is interesting is that boat funerals were not reserved solely for males;boat funerals were a tradition practiced for both male and female deceased Vikings.

According to a report from Ahmad ibn Fadlan, a middle ages-traveler, one instance of the notorious boat funeral was for a Viking chieftain, which included a female slave as a sacrifice who would be cremated at sea with her master. The scenes that were said to follow were truly horrific and unimaginably barbaric. According to Ahmad, the female slave was forced to drink alcohol to such levels of severe alcohol poisoning. However, the alcohol would not be what killed her, as immediately after she was raped by every man in the village in the name of tribute for the deceased chieftain. After being raped countless times, she was strangled and stabbed to death by the deceased's wife, who at the time was known as the "Angel of Death." Finally, the slave would be placed on the vessel with her master and set alight from a fiery arrow shot from an archer's hand (Morgan, 2018).

There were many variations in the Viking Age when it came to disposing of and honoring the dead; however, regardless of how the dead were to be honored, the fallen Vikings would still practice a few rituals that would remain untouched no matter how the body was disposed of. One of these practices included dressing the deceased in brand new clothes that would be created specifically for the funeral. Another tradition was that at the funeral service, a ceremony was always held, which would always include food, alcohol, chants, and traditional songs.

At these ceremonies, gifts were also ever present, and they were offered as tribute in honor of the fallen Vikings. These gifts were known as 'grave goods' and generally consisted of items that were equal to the dead Viking's economic status. These would often include things such as garments, weapons, jewelry, and occasionally, slaves. The 'grave goods' would either be buried with the deceased or burned at the pyre if the Viking was cremated.

Recently, a Viking site was discovered in Flakstad, Norway. At this gravesite it was found that there were multiple bodies laid to rest together in a single grave. Some of these were even decapitated. After studies and a DNA analysis had been done, it was determined that the bodies were in fact slaves who had been sacrificed to spend their eternal slumber with their owner even in death. (Morgan, 2018).

Warding Off Draugr

Just as the Vikings would honor the dead and assist the dead on their travels to Valhalla, the Norsemen were also wary of the draugr. Draugr, also known as aptrgangr in Old Norse, were the equivalent of modern-day zombies at the time of the Viking Age. According to experts, it was believed that once a person was buried, it was possible that the departed corpse could be reanimated again. The corpse was believed to live innocently in its grave, protecting the goods and treasures they were buried with from grave robbers. These innocent undead corpses were known as hangbui. However, if the hangbui's goods were stolen by grave robbers, they would turn into a draugr. When a hangbui turned into a draugr, they would borrow out of their eternal resting spot into the world of the living and harm any man, woman, or child that crossed its path (Esser, 2018).

In order to prevent this catastrophe from unfolding, the Norsemen took many precautions when burning the deceased's body. The Vikings would place many pieces of straw in the shape of crosses under the shroud, as well as a pair of scissors that were opened across the chest on those who had since passed. The Vikings were believed to have tied corpses' big toes together and hammer nails into the soles of their feet so that if the dead were to arise and go on a rampage, they would not be able to walk.

How the coffin was carried and lowered into the grave was also significant. When the Vikings carried the coffin out of the deceased's house, the coffin bearers would cautiously come to a halt. Before exiting the door of the deceased's house, the bearers would lower and raise the coffin in three movements in different directions, creating the shape of a cross. According to experts, sometimes the body would be carried out through a specific door known as the 'corpse-door,' which was a hole in the wall covered in bricks. The corpse door was specifically designed to only be exited once someone had died and would be torn open to remove the dead and then be put back together once the deceased had been buried.

The corpse-door may seem incredibly unnecessary without context; however, according to experts, it is believed that Vikings thought that the deceased could only return into a building in the same entrance they came out of. Due to this logic, once a corpse-door had been reassembled, the draugr wouldn't be able to enter the house again. The Vikings' fear of the draugr went even further. The deceased's corpse would carefully be carried out with their feet coming out of the door first so that its head would be facing away from the path the coffin bearers took to the burial mound. This was done so the corpse would not be able to memorize the path back from where it came if the deceased were to turn into a ferocious draugr. Once buried, a magic spell was meant to be said at the gravesite to bind the deceased to their eternal grave.

Lastly, once the coffin had safely and cautiously been moved out of the house, then every jar, saucepan, cutlery, crockery, chair, and stool recently used by the deceased were to be turned upside down (Esser, 2018).

Wedding Ceremonies

The Vikings believed in holy matrimony and the sacred bond between man and wife. Just like Christians and other religious followers, the Vikings also partook in the act of marriage and was practiced by almost the entire adult population of the Norsemen. Before a woman was to be married to a male Viking, they would wear a kransen. A Kransen was a gilt circlet that was won by all unwed Viking women, along with their being worn loose. However, during a wedding ceremony, the bride would remove her kransen and would replace it with a Viking wedding crown. The bride's kransen would then become a family heirloom. The kransen would be passed down to her future daughter, then to her granddaughter, and eventually be passed down from generation to generation to all the women of the bride's bloodline (Esser, 2018).

With regards to the groom, he would acquire a sword from one of his ancestors that had been passed down from generation to generation. Some experts believe that there was a possibility that the sword had been recovered by breaking into the grave of their dead ancestors and taking the sword that they had been buried with. Other opinions on the matter suggest that a fake grave was prepared for occasions like a wedding, which would be broken into to obtain the sword the groom would be presented with. However, regardless of the methods of how the groom obtained the sword, the protocol at the wedding ceremony was the same. During the wedding ceremony, the groom would carry the sword and sometimes even a hammer to symbolize the god of thunder, Thor. What is interesting is that neither the groom nor the bride had special clothes allocated for them to wear for the wedding; they wore the same clothes they would have worn on a regular day.

A Viking wedding was always held on a Friday. Friday was Frigg's day; Frigg was the wife of Odin and the goddess of fertility. The ceremony would always begin by attempting to garner the attention of the Norse gods by dedicating a sacrifice in the form of an animal in honor of Frigg, Odin, and the other gods.

After the sacrifice, the bride and the groom would meet at the altar. The groom would present the sword of his ancestors to his soon-to-be wife as an heirloom that would be passed on to their firstborn son. The bride would give the groom another sword as a token of their marriage to be used to protect their future family from any danger. Once the bride and the groom had exchanged swords, it was time for the soon-to-be newlyweds to exchange rings and vows (Esser, 2018).

The bride and the groom would exchange a kiss, and the two would officially be named husband and wife in the name of the gods. After the ceremony, all who had attended would make their way to the hall to feast on a seemingly endless supply of meat, fish, alcohol, and all sorts of delicious food. It would be here in the hall where everyone was feasting that the groom would assist the bride over the threshold and thrust his sword with all his strength into a pillar. It was believed that the deeper the groom managed to plunge his sword unto the wooden pillar, the more children and luck would be bestowed upon the married couple by the gods. Furthermore, it was customary that the newlyweds would share bridal ale, which was usually mead, every night for the next month.

Lastly, after everyone had eaten and the ceremony had come to a close, one last tradition needed to be upheld. The couple would be accompanied to bed by a few of the guests who attended the wedding to act as witnesses so they could testify that the union between husband and wife had been consummated. The morning after the marriage had been consummated, the bride would tie up her hair and would cover it with a cloth to showcase her new status of being a wife to the rest of the village. The groom would finally hand over the keys to his house to his new wife and they would continue their lives as a happily married couple (Esser, 2018).

Infant Rituals and Naming Ceremonies

Within Norse mythology, when a baby was born, there were a handful of rituals that needed to be practiced before the infant child could be considered a real person in Viking society. Before these rituals had been completed, the baby Norseman could not be considered a human being yet. According to experts, it was likely a defense mechanism that the Vikings had adopted to protect themselves emotionally, as the infant mortality rate was dangerously high. If the infant wasn't considered human yet, then the death of a baby was far less emotionally taxing in the minds of the Viking parents at the time.

So in order to emotionally protect the parents, infant rituals were put in place. When a Viking baby was born, the infant would be placed on the ground until his/her Viking father picked up the child and placed the infant inside of his coat. Placing the child inside of the father's coat would symbolize that the father had accepted the infant as his own child. Once the father had done this, he would then inspect if the infant had any physical problems. If the child was found to have any problems from birth, the child would be left exposed and unattended until the baby died. However, if the child was found to have no birth defects, a ceremony would be held known as ausa vatni. During ausa vatni, water would be sprinkled over the baby, similar to baptism in Christianity (Esser, 2018).

Once the ceremony had concluded and the baby was found to be healthy and accepted by its father, a naming ceremony would commence known as nafnfesti. During nafnfesti, the father would provide his newborn baby with a gift and name the child. The gift that most infants received during nafnfesti would generally be a ring, a weapon, or a farm/land deed that they would receive when the child grew older. Once the ausa vanti and nafnfesti ceremonies were completed, the child was accepted by the Viking community and was officially considered a human being. The child could no longer be subject to harm or exposure to the elements, as this would, from this point on, be considered murder (Esser, 2018).

Chapter 4: The Gods of Norse Mythology

The Aesir gods made up a large portion of the Norse pantheon. The word pantheon can be understood as a collective group of gods within a particular culture; for example, there would be the Egyptian pantheon or the Greek Pantheon that would consist of those regions' collective gods. The word pantheon comes from the Greek words pan (all) and theoi (gods), thus suggesting all the gods of a particular group or belief system. The Norse pantheon consisted of the Aesir, Vanir, jötnar, and many other minor deities and demigods. Thus, the Norse pantheon consisted of a wide range of deities and divine beings who were responsible for and controlled different sections of the nine realms of the cosmos.

However, the list of the Norse pantheon is incredibly lengthy and is made up of many different bloodlines and races, making it difficult to single out every Norse god of the time. Thus, in order to truly grasp the Norse pantheon, it is best to highlight only the most important gods and goddesses that the Norsemen worshipped during the Viking age.

The Norse pantheon can be divided into three major groups. These groups consist of the Aesir (the newest generation of gods), the Vanir (the old gods), and the jötnar (the giants who inhabited the universe first). However, only the most important of these gods will be discussed. After years of bloodshed between these three groups, the Aesir would come out victorious and be the most powerful gods who would rule the cosmos (Gill, 2019).

Odin

Odin, also known as Woden in Old English, is the father of all the gods and mortals and rules over Asgard, home of the Aesir. Odin is married to Frigg, the goddess of love and war, and has many children, most notably Thor, Baldur, and Vidar. In the Marvel comics, Loki is his adopted son, but in mythology, Loki is occasionally referred to as his half-brother.

Odin would sit on his throne, known as Hlidskjalf, inside the safety of Valhalla's gates, where he would observe tirelessly over the nine realms of the cosmos. Odin is the god of war, however, he is also associated as the god of magic, wisdom, poetry, and the runic alphabet (Gods and Goddesses, 2017). Odin often appears in many heroic pieces of literature, written at the time of the Vikings, as the protector of heroes. What this means is that Odin admired and protected warriors who had fallen in the name of battle and would welcome them into the gates of Valhalla, Odin's palatial home with 640 doors. Odin and his wife Frigg would possess the souls of the warriors who had been slain in battle. The half that belonged to Odin would enter Valhalla for their final resting place, where they would feast, indulge in fornication, and engage in as much battle as their heart's content. The fallen warriors would be met by Odin's daughters, the valkyrie, and would be transported to the heavenly realm of Asgard; those who were not worthy would be transported to Helheim (Britannica, 2018).

Odin valued knowledge and always sought out ways to further it. He was intently captivated by the runes, the letters of the runic alphabet. Odin was so interested to seek out further knowledge from the ancient runic alphabet that he hung himself from a tree with a spear impaled in his side for nine days and nine nights with no food or water and vowed to himself that he would only come down from the torture until he unlocked the secret of the runes. Eventually, after nine full days and nights, the All-Father unlocked the secrets of the runes and would often use them to practice his wizardry, for which he was highly esteemed for.

However, Odin's quest for wisdom and knowledge never ceased, and he would search for new ways to improve upon these qualities no matter the cost. Odin even lost his eye in search of true never-ending wisdom. Odin sacrificed his eye so that he could drink from Urd's (well of wisdom located by Yggdrasil). His eye was the price he had to pay to convince the giant Mimir to provide him with a drink from the well out of a horn. However, Odin's sacrifice did pay off, and he profited with eternal wisdom. Odin would also steal the head of Mimir, the giant that offered him the drink from Urd's well when Vanir decapitated the giant, as Odin believed that Mirmir's severed head would tell him the secrets of the universe and provide him with advice (Gods and Goddesses, 2017).

In art, Odin was depicted as a tall, old man with a full white beard and would always be shown as having only one eye, as his other eye was traded for enhanced wisdom. Odin would normally be seen wearing a cloak and a large wide-brimmed hat. The god of war would generally be depicted with a spear, known as Gungnir, which he received from his adopted son Loki, the god of mischief, after he stole it from a group of dwarves who created it. Odin sometimes was depicted with two ravens by his side who were known as Hugin (thought) and Munin (memory). These ravens were Odin's companions, and he would send them across the nine worlds to bring back intel and stories of what they saw in the rest of the cosmos. In art, Odin is also often accompanied by his two pet wolves Geri and Freki. Odin created these wolves due to being lonely. Odin would send Freki and Geri to bloody battlefields to feed off the corpses of the fallen warriors. Odin is the god of all gods in Norse mythology, and was generally honored above all the other gods (Gods and Goddesses, 2017).

Frigg

The word Frigg can be translated to 'beloved' in Old Norse, which is incredibly fitting, as the goddess of love was definitely the most beloved goddess of the Norsemen, as she was the Queen of the Aesir and the loving wife of the All-Father Odin. Frigg was a goddess considered to represent many aspects of the human condition and reality, and the Norsemen believed Frigg to be the goddess of love, fertility, marriage, and war. However, it does not stop there. In many regions of Scandinavia, Frigg was also considered to represent fate, foresight, and wisdom. It was often believed that Frigg could see one's fate and could see into the future. Frigg was also a sky goddess and was responsible for weaving the clouds, as well as weaving the fates of mortals. It is believed that Frigg would use the clouds to weave garments for the Aesir gods. Frigg was a motherly figure to all the Norse pantheon, as well as to the Vikings that worshiped her.

What is interesting is that Friday is named after the goddess, Frigg, and Wednesday is named after her husband the All-Father, Odin (Woden in Old English), and to this day, the names have never changed and the origins of these days of the week remain true. What's more, the god of lightning, Thor, also has a day of the week named in his honor, which is Thursday, also known as "Thor's day." This shows how renowned these gods were even outside of Scandinavia, and that the name of these days was used even in England, the nation that hated the Vikings more than anybody.

Frigg had many responsibilities, which was to be expected with a goddess of her stature. One of the goddess's most important duties was to oversee all of the mortal marriages sanctioned in society, and was a beacon of shining light to the Vikings and highly admired and worshiped during matrimonies. In fact, during the Viking Age, it was sanctioned that you could only be married on a Friday. This was because Friday, as mentioned earlier, was the day that was specifically reserved in honor of the goddess Frigg. Due to this, Frigg was seen as the protector of the Norsemen's homes and families, and brought good fortune to those who were married.

As Queen of the Aesir and Asgard, it was only natural that the Norse women of Scandinavia would view the goddess of love, marriage, and fertility as their role model and a figure they strived to imitate in their daily lives. Frigg was often called upon by her female followers for aid in the domestic arts and cottage industry, as it was believed that the goddess herself would partake in these activities due to her perceived kind, gentle, and loving nature.

Another responsibility of this goddess was to ensure that peace and social order in the cosmos was maintained. According to legend, whenever the Aesir gods had a feast, Frigg would be present and she would always be carrying a horn filled with mead. At these feasts, she would do one of two things: she would either welcome warriors back from battle or she would give them one last meal before sending them off to battle. Thus, Frigg was sometimes referred to by her nickname 'lady of the hall,' which led to the goddess of marriage being associated as a patroness of diplomacy (Ancient Origins, 2019).

However, as Frigg was the goddess of fertility, she was also a mother herself. In Scandinavia at the time of the Vikings, the longest night of the year was known as 'Mother Night,' and was believed to be the night that the goddess Frigg gave birth to her son Baldur, the god of light and joy (Ancient Origins, 2019). Frigg was a fantastic mother and was incredibly loving and nurturing to her son; however, ill fate awaited Baldur, and Frigg knew this. As mentioned earlier, Frigg is also the goddess of prophecy, and as such, she foresaw in a dream that her child would have an untimely death.

Unfortunately, she could not save her son, and Baldur lost his life, regardless of her multiple efforts to try and avoid it. Frigg was believed to never be the same after her son's death, but remained the goddess of love, marriage, and fertility to the Norsemen and was beloved and honored by all.

Baldur

Baldur is the god of all that is good and is associated with all that is beautiful and joyous in the cosmos. Baldur was the second son of Odin and Frigg and the younger twin sibling of his blind brother Hodr. Like his mother Frigg, Baldur was a very friendly, kind, and loving god; however, he was not particularly mighty or powerful, nor was he bestowed with the great strength and physical prowess like his half-siblings, such as Thor, had been gifted with (P. Geller, 2016b).

However, despite this, everybody loved Baldur, and he was one of the most loved gods in all of Asgard. Whoever Baldur spent time with, or wherever the son of Frigg went, joy was inevitably going to be experienced by all.

As said earlier, it was prophesied that Baldur would meet an untimely demise, and no matter how hard his parents tried to prevent it, the result would end in tragedy. However, this was not with a lack of effort. Odin and Frigg would not accept this fate, and thus, Odin took it upon himself to seek out a solution. Odin traveled to Helheim (the underworld) where a deceased female seer resided. Odin would disguise himself, but would find that Helheim had been decorated for an event of celebration. It turned out that the seeress that resided in Helheim was aware of the prophecy regarding Baldur's death, and that the residents of Helheim were preparing a party in Baldur's honor, as they wanted to welcome the arrival of such an esteemed guest of Baldur's divine status.

Horrified from what he witnessed, Odin told Frigg about what had been prophesied in Helheim and what would befall their son. Frigg was terrified, and she visited every living thing in the cosmos and got an oath from everybody that no harm would befall her son.

With this new collective oath, Baldur was considered essentially invincible. The other gods of Asgard found this incredibly amusing and decided to play a game. The game entailed throwing all sorts of things at Baldur to watch them bounce off the god of joy harmlessly.

Loki, the god of mischief, saw this as an opportunity to bring upon chaos. Loki lived for chaos and mischief, as it entertained him immensely. Loki disguised himself and went over to Frigg and asked the goddess if she truly got an oath from EVERY living thing in the universe. Frigg carelessly let slip that she failed to gain the oath from the mistletoe, as she could not see any harm that it could bring upon her son.

Armed with this new and exciting knowledge, the god of mischief went over to Hodr, Baldur's blind brother, and asked if he wanted to join in throwing objects at his now invincible brother. Hodr accepted and Loki gave the blind brother a sharpened branch of the mistletoe that Frigg failed to get an oath from and pointed Hodr in the right direction of his brother. Hodr launched the branch and struck Baldur dead on the spot (P. Geller, 2016b).

Thor

Thor is the son of Odin and is the god of thunder. Thor was one of the most popular gods in Norse mythology, and was even more popular than Odin himself in some regions during the Viking Age. Thor's popularity grew in stature at the expense of his father Odin in the 9th century. This is because many farmers would flee Norway for a safer life in Iceland in order to escape the tyrannical and oppressive rule of the Norwegian king, who worshiped Odin. Due to this, Thor's popularity reached its peak from around the years 790-1066 during the Viking Age (Gods and Goddesses, 2016).

Thor has become widely popular in the modern era through his portrayals in pop culture, most notably his depiction in Marvel comics and the Marvel cinematic universe. However, with regards to Norse mythology, Thor was the god of thunder. He was also associated as being the protector of mankind. Thor is widely recognizable for wielding his hammer Mjölnir (Mjǫllnir in Old Norse), which he used to control the lighting, thunder, and storms. Thor was regarded as the most powerful of the Norse gods and was renowned for being incredibly strong. Due to this, he was feared by many. Many mortals feared Thor due to his immense power, but had the utmost admiration for him, as they knew he was interested in preserving the wellbeing and happiness of mankind.

Thor represented many aspects of the human condition. It is believed that the god of Thunder symbolized the three main pillars of manhood, as well as being associated as being the god of fertility. These pillars included the ability to provide for your loved ones, protect those who are dear to you, and procreation. Thor was not necessarily known as a god who was loving or gentle, but it was a collective belief that Thor had a good heart and always had pure intentions. Thor would use his overwhelming strength to protect the people around him. Thor was known to be a prideful god, and thus would protect his own honor, as well as the honor of others. Thor was the ultimate defender of justice and balance of the cosmos, unlike his half-brother Loki. Thor was married to the goddess Sif. The exact details of Thor's lineage are blurry; however, based on accounts, it is evident that Thor had at least three children, Thrud, Magni, and Jarnsaxa, and was a supportive and nurturing father (Geller, 2017).

Thor's greatest enemies were the jötnar who lived in Jotunheim, as well as the ginormous sea serpent known as Jormungand. Jormungand represented all that was evil and was a beast that needed to be slain. According to Edda, which is a body of ancient Icelandic literature that has served as the primary source and basis of what the modern world knows of Norse mythology, Thor and Jormungand fought on two occasions. The most notable of the two was a battle that depicts a scene where Thor virtually pulls the sea serpent straight out the ocean; however, at the last minute, Thor was stopped by the jotunn Hymir, who believed that if Thor plucked Jormungand from the ocean, it would lead to the end of the cosmos. Thor listened and restrained from slaying the sea serpent. According to legend, Thor and the Jormungand will fight again during Ragnarok and both will end up killing one another (Gods and Goddesses, 2016).

Thor's appearance is actually much different from that of his modern portrayal in Marvel comics and films. Thor was believed to have long flowing red hair and a full red beard. He was always portrayed as a very strong and muscular man, leaving no secret of his immense strength based on his build. Most artistic representations of the god of thunder depict him with a ferocious appearance, yet despite his intimidating stature and aesthetic, he remained among the gods of the Norse pantheon. Unlike Odin, Thor did not accept any human sacrifices. This only added to the Norse god's lovable reputation.

Heimdallr

Heimdallr, or Heimdallrr in Old Norse, was considered to be the watchman and messenger of all the gods. Heimdallr is often described as being the fairest or whitest-skinned of all the Norse pantheon, and is why he is sometimes referred to as the Shining God. Heimdallr dwelled at the entry gates of Asgard and guarded over the Bifrost bridge, which was a rainbow-colored bridge that connected Asgard to all the other eight realms of the cosmos. Bifrost was so enormous that it could be seen from anywhere in all the realms of the cosmos. In Old Norse, the word bifask can be translated to the English word 'tremble,' and the röst can be translated to mean 'mile.' Thus, Bifrost directly translates to the 'trembling mile' (Skjalden, 2020b).

Heimdallr was tasked to guard Bifrost with his life and keep Asgard safe from any enemy frontiers or intruders. Due to Heimdallr guarding the Bifrost, he was also regarded as the symbol of the preservation of the cosmos and acted as the communication link between the gods, goddesses, and mankind.

Heimdallr was an incredibly powerful god and possessed heightened physical abilities that surpassed almost all of the gods; this is why he was entrusted to guard something as important as the Bifrost to ensure the safety of Asgard. Heimdallr was believed to need less sleep than a bird and possessed the ability to see his surroundings from hundreds of kilometers away. His hearing was as impressive as his sight, as it was said Heimdallr could hear grass that was growing in meadows and hear wool that grew on sheep. These were excellent qualities to have and perfectly suited for the guard of Asgard. Heimdallr would sound his horn, known as Gjallarhorn, if he felt Asgard was being ambushed or the kingdom of the Aesir was in danger. However, he would only sound Gjallarhorn when he felt it was absolutely necessary. If a jotunn were to be so foolish as to launch an attack on Asgard or sneak into the realm of the Aesir, then Heimdallr would use his sword, known as Hofund, to slay the enemies and intruders. However, it was extremely unlikely that the jötnar would be able to launch an attack on Asgard, as they were unlikely able to make their way up the Bifrost anyway. The rainbow bridge was constantly on fire, and thus, it was too hot to be on the bridge itself. It is said that the Bifrost always had a red glow to it due to the heat radiating off of it (Britannica, 2019a).

It is believed that when Heimdallr blows on Gjallarhorn, it can be heard throughout heaven, earth, and the lower realms. According to legend, Heimdallr will sound Gjallarhorn to signal the beginning of Ragnarok and use it as an alarm to summon the Aesir to form an army to fight their enemies to the death. It is said that during Ragnarok, Heimdallr would engage in battle with Loki, and the two gods would wind up killing one another.

Loki

Loki was the god of mischief, but is also sometimes considered the god of fire. Loki was a trickster god by nature and was never considered to be either good or evil, as although he caused terrible trouble for both mortals and the gods, he would also sometimes use his cunning, wits, and slyness for the wellbeing of the gods and mortals. Loki would often be represented as the trusted companion of the great gods Odin and Thor; however, Loki's main ambition in life was to create chaos. No matter who was affected by his schemes was irrelevant to him.

Unlike many other gods in the Norse pantheon, historians have managed to decipher the meaning of Loki's name and its origin. In Old Norse, the noun 'loki' can be translated to the English word 'tangle.' This is significant, as tangle had the connotation of knots, chaos, and scheming, which would symbolize Loki's ability to tangle up the lives of others and rope them into his treacherous and mischievous plots.

Loki was not your typical god and he was not a blood relative of the Aesir tribe. This is because Loki's father was actually a jotunn known as Farbauti, and his mother was Laufey, who is sometimes considered a god and other times considered a jotunn herself. However, Loki was astray from his parents, was known to spend most of his life in the realm of Asgard, and was even often considered an Aesir, despite his jotunn heritage. Some believe that Loki was even the adopted son of Odin; however, some sources deny this claim.

Loki had a romantic relationship with the jotunn Angrboda and had three children with the giant. Their children included Loki's daughter Hel, who rules over Helheim (the underworld), the enormous sea serpent Jormungand, who was prophesied to kill Thor during Ragnarok, and their third child Fenrir, who was a ferocious wolf.

However, Loki would go on to marry the goddess Sigu, and the couple would have a son named Nari. Loki also had the power to shapeshift, and as expected, he would use this ability to scheme cunning plans and cause immense chaos in the cosmos. On one occasion, Loki even shapeshifted into a beautiful woman and seduced Odin, and he would go on to become the mother of Sleipnir, who was Odin's trusted horse.

As mentioned earlier in the chapter, Loki was responsible for the death of Aesir's favorite son Baldur. The gods of the Aesir found out that Loki was indeed the schemer behind the murder. When Baldur died, Loki immediately began to laugh, which was a testament to his guilt and role in the death of Odin's son. Loki knew immediately that the Aesir knew he was to blame, so he began to flee; however, he was caught and the gods came up with a fitting punishment. The Aesir removed the intestines of one of Loki's sons and used those intestines to tie the god of mischief to a rock. Loki would be sentenced to spend the rest of eternity tied to this rock while a cobra would spit burning venom on his face for the rest of his days.

In art, the god of mischief Loki would generally be portrayed as donning a jester-like appearance, with many artistic representations depicting Loki dancing and sneering. Loki's nose is generally represented as being unusually large; however, what is interesting about Loki is that you will find many depictions of his appearance, as Loki could shapeshift and alter his appearance as he pleased.

Freya

Freya was one of the principal goddesses of the Norse pantheon; however, she was not born an Aesir goddess but instead of the Vanir tribe. Although she was born of the Vanir tribe, she lived in harmony with the Aesir in Asgard for most of her life. Freya was the goddess of blessings, lust, love, beauty, and fertility. Due to Freya being born from the Vanir tribe, she shared her tribe's penchant for magical arts. Freya was the goddess that introduced the magic known as *seidr* to the Aesir gods, which would eventually lead to the Vanir and Aesir war. The Vanir and Aesir war will be discussed in Chapter 6. Freya's seidr magic would allow their practitioners to have knowledge of the future, and armed with that knowledge, the future could be changed (Mythopedia, 2018).

In nature, Freya was more agreeable than other Norse gods and goddesses. For example, where Thor would achieve his goals through brute strength and Loki would achieve his ambitions through trickery, Freya would achieve her objectives through gentler persuasion with the help of her beauty, offering sex, and gifts. Frey was generally considered as being an unselfish and helpful goddess; however, she also had a dark side. Similar to the males of the Norse pantheon, Freya had a taste for blood and was said to be a fierce warrior who would fight valiantly in battle. According to myths, it is said that Frey took countless lives of warriors in battle (Mythopedia, 2018).

While Freya was not known to typically fight with weapons, she was known to possess countless spells and powerful magi to aid her in battle. On top of that, Freya possessed many assortments of various different types. One of the most significant of these assortments included a cloak made out of falcon feathers, which would allow the goddess the gift of flight; however, the cloak did not just give Freya the power. Anyone who wore it would have this power also. It is said that when Freya was not using this cloak, she would lend it to many companions and collaborators who agreed to her bidding. However, although this cloak was extremely powerful, it was not her most prized possession.

The possession that Freya considered to be all-important was a necklace known as Brísingamen. Brísingamen was forged by dwarves, and the goddess purchased this necklace at a dear price. It is said she would constantly guard this necklace and would kill any soul who dared take it from her. However, Brísingamen and the cloak made of falcon wings were not the only possessions she cherished. This included the goddess's glittering chariot, which was pulled by two black domesticated cats. Freya would also generally be accompanied by an animal familiar, which was a boar known as Hildisvín, which translates to battle swine. Freya was a significant goddess in the Norse pantheon and was loved by many (Mythopedia, 2018).

Chapter 5: The Poems of the Poetic and Prose Edda

The poems of Edda are a godsend for historians, and are the primary sources in which historians have been able to piece together the Viking era and Norse mythology as we know it today. Due to the Viking culture being one of an oral society rather than that of a written one, a lot of the secrets, customs, and beliefs of the time have been lost to history due to the lack of documentation. However, thanks to the Prose Edda and the Poetic Edda, some light has been brought on the history of the Vikings.

The Prose Edda was a text of old Norse Poetics, which was written around the year 1200 by an Icelandic poet by the name of Snorri Sturlson. Snorri compiled an anthology of poems that provide the world with a large variety of lore, which shed light on what life in Scandinavia during the time of the Vikings was like. The text itself is incredibly beneficial from an educational standpoint as it provided a consistent narrative of many of the plotlines of Norse mythology that had been lacking before the introduction of the poems of Edda. Snorri did not believe in Norse mythology himself; in fact, he was a Christian. However, he treated the ancient pagan mythology with the utmost professionalism and respect. Thanks to Snorri, a quasi-historical backstory of the Norse pantheon was developed. What was so significant about the Prose Edda was that Snorri documented one of the first attempts to devise a rational explanation from the supernatural and legendary events that unfolded from the perception of mythology (Sacred Texts, 2019).

The Poetic Edda was written slightly later than Snorri's Prose Edda and is dated back to the second half of the 13th century. However, the Poetic Edda contains even older materials than the Prose Edda, and as a result, is sometimes known as the Elder Edda, even though it was written after the Prose Edda. The Poetic Edda is a collection of epic poems that highlight the mythological beliefs of the Viking age between the years 800-1100; however, the authorship of the Poetic Edda is unknown, unlike the Prose Edda (Britannica, 2019a).

Nevertheless, the Poetic Edda is the collection of evidence that historians of today rely on to a larger degree, as it is the largest source of information regarding Norse mythology to date. The revolutionary poems that are found in the pages of the Poetic Edda usually consist of short dramatic dialogues and simple archaic writing styles, which beautifully portray the poetry of the skalds (poets) of ancient times. The poems in the Poetic Edda highlight the iconic stories of Thor, Odin, Loki, Frigg, and the other Norse gods and goddesses, the jötnar, Vanir, and other magical creatures.

The Poem of Vafþrúðnismál (Vafthundnir's Sayings)

This poem of the collection of the Poetic Edda in the *in-Codex Regius,* the All-Father Odin's obsession for knowledge is truly highlighted. In the poem of Vafþrúðnismál, Odin sets forth to search for further knowledge about himself and the cosmos by venturing to the home of the jotunn Vafthundnir. Odin's wife Frigg is frightened and tries with all her effort to persuade Odin to give up on his venture for knowledge as she fears the jotunn Vafthundnir may be too dangerous and too powerful for even the All-Father to handle alone. However, Odin refused to listen, dismissed all of Frigg's claims, and left to go and test the jotunn's wisdom.

Upon Odin's arrival at the hall in which Vafthundnir resides, Odin cleverly disguised himself as a man known by the name as Gagnrad, so that the jotunn would not be able to recognize the mighty god of war. Gagnrad asked Vafthundnir if he was merely wise or very wise and challenged the jotunn to a game of wits. Vafthundnir accepted and invited the stranger in to entertain his request. Thus ,Odin and the jotunn began their battle to see who was wiser (Book Rags, 2018).

Odin originally planned to simply have a friendly Q&A with the jotunn; however, Vafthundnir was far too prideful and competitive for that. Instead, Vafthundnir proposed that the two engage in a game with much higher stakes. The jotunn proposed that the loser of this battle of wits should be decapitated and disposed of. However, Vafthundnir did not realize he was dealing with Odin, and to little surprise, the god of war accepted the jotunn's terms.

Odin suggested that, as Vafthundnir's guest, he should be asked the questions first. The jotunn agreed and asked Odin a series of questions. The two would go on and ask each other questions one after the other and both of them would continue to get them correct. However, after some time, Odin found the answer that he had been searching for, which was how he was prophesied to die. Now that Odin was armed with this knowledge, he grew bored and would ask a question only he knew the answer to. The question he asked was, "What did Odin whisper to his dead son?" At that point, Vafthundnir knew he was not playing a game of wits with Gagnrad, but with Odin instead. The jotunn could not answer Odin's question, and as agreed upon earlier, the loser would be decapitated. Odin had gained the knowledge he had been searching for and Vafthundnir lost his life (From Baker to Edlund, 2014).

The Poem of Þrymskviða (Thrym's Poem)

The poem of Þrymskviða, also known as Thrym's poem, is a comical one and a very interesting take of the Norse pantheon, who are so often associated with blood and warfare. There is still death in this poem; however, it is a rather amusing and charming part of Norse lore.

The poem begins with Thor's iconic hammer, Mjölnir, being stolen by the jotunn Thrym, also known as Þrymr in Old Norse. The jotunn tells Thor that the only way he will return Mjölnir is if the goddess Frigg is offered to him in marriage as payment for it. Thor, desperate to get the all-powerful Mjölnir back in his possession, tries to convince Frigg to marry Thrym; however, unsurprisingly, the goddess refuses. Thor needed to get creative and sought help from the god of mischief, Loki. Loki found this hilarious, but nonetheless provided Thor with an 'ingenious' scheme to get Mjölnir back. Thor agreed and went along with Loki's ridiculous plan. Instead of Frigg being offered to Thrym, the Aesir would trick the jotunn and offer Thor in an Aesir dress. Thor would act as the bride, and Loki Thor's bridesmaid. The two gods would travel to Jötunheim for the wedding, starting their quest to retrieve Mjölnir.

Thor's identity is hilariously hinted at throughout the reception. Thor was not shy at the reception either; it is stated that he ate an entire ox on his own. Loki somehow managed to cunningly provide very shallow explanations to the giants regarding the odd behavior of the soon-to-be wife 'Frigg,' and miraculously, the giants accepted these explanations to be true. It is stated that Loki claimed that the bride's unimaginable hunger was due to her not eating for seven days because she was simply too excited for the wedding that she couldn't stomach anything. However, the wedding ceremony continued and Mjölnir eventually landed in Thor's hands. This was part of the tradition in which the bride and groom are meant to present one another with a weapon. Now that Mjölnir was safely given back to the thunder god, he used it to strike down the jotunn and return back home to Asgard (The Honest Modern Heathen, 2020).

The Poem of Hymiskviða (The Lay of Hymir)

In the poem of Hymiskviða, an epic story of Thor's acquisition of the jotunn Hymir's cauldron is told. This type of poem is the stuff of legends and is the kind of story you would tell your children at bedtime.

The poem begins with the gods of Asgard searching for an eternal source of mead in which they demanded to be provided to them by

Aegir (Ægir in Old Norse), the god of the ocean. However, Aegir was not impressed with the tone of the request from the gods, and thus, the god of the ocean would supply the gods with endless mead if they could supply Aegir with a cauldron large enough to hold their unimaginable request. This enormous vessel was incredibly scarce, and very few were known to be in existence. However, Tyr, the god of war and justice, knew how they could obtain this enormous cauldron. According to Tyr, his father Hymir, who was an enormous jötunn, owned a cauldron that was described to be a 'league deep.' To put that into perspective, that would mean that the cauldron was three and a half miles in size, which would be the perfect vessel to entice Aegir to supply the Aesir gods with an endless supply of mead. Though Tyr knew his father Hymir would not be so willing to hand over his enormous cauldron without a fight. The god of war enlisted Thor to aid him in tricking Hymir into handing it over through deception.

Thus, Tyr and Thor began their quest and ventured forth to pay a visit to the jötunn, Hymir. The journey to Hymir was long and full of adventure. The two gods even participated in a fishing trip in which Thor caught two enormous whales he planned to give Hymir as a gift. However, even though Thor presented his gift to the jötunn, Hymir still was not warming up to his guests. Hymir tells Thor, "Sure, you may be able to row a boat well, but if you are really strong, you should be able to prove it by breaking this glass goblet." Hymir would offer his enormous cauldron as a prize if Thor could break the goblet. Thor accepted Hymir's proposal. He took the goblet from the hands of Hymir and smashed it with all his strength against a stone pillar. However, the glass goblet was still completely intact without a scratch while the stone pillar crumbled to pieces.

It is said in the poem that Hymir's wife provided Thor with some advice and told the thunder god to instead smash the goblet on Hymir's head, as it was far harder than the glass goblet. Thor accepted the advice he was given and the goblet shattered on the jötunn's head. Hymir was saddened that his prized goblet had been shattered; however, he stuck to his word and rewarded Thor with the cauldron that the Aesir gods were searching for. However, Hymir said, "You may only take the cauldron if you can carry it."

Tyr could barely make the cauldron budge; however, Thor managed to carry it with ease, so the two gods left Hymir's palace. Tyr and Thor did not get very far before Hymir had a change of heart and decided he wanted the cauldron back. Having just taken a few steps, the pair of gods looked behind them only to see Hymir and troops of his multi-headed henchmen coming to reclaim the jötunn's prized possession by force. Thor put down the cauldron steadily on the floor, pulled out his trusty hammer, and dispatched all of the pursuers and Hymir with relative ease. Once the pair of gods knew that the cauldron was safely in their possession, they would journey back home to Asgard.

Tyr and Thor returned, and the rest of the Aesir gods were extremely pleased with the pair and the successful quest of obtaining the cauldron needed for the mead the gods so desired. Even the god of the ocean, Aegir, was overjoyed and full of praise. Aegir changed his tone towards the Aesir's initial request and began to cheerfully brew up an unimaginable quantity of mead to last the Aesir through the winter (Kissell, 2018).

The Poem of Skírnismál (Skirnir's Journey)

This poem is a story of love, and unrequited love at that. The poem begins with Freyr, the god of kinship, good harvest, sunshine, peace, fertility, and prosperity. Freyr decides it upon himself to take a seat on Odin's throne within the gates of Valhalla, even though he knows he is not supposed to. On the throne, Freyr is able to view all the nine realms of the cosmos. Freyr's gaze is drawn to North Jotunheim, in which the god of peace and prosperity feasts his eyes on the great jötunn, Gymir. As Freyr casually gazes upon Gymir's halls, he sees Gymnir's astonishingly beautiful jötunn daughter by the name of Grid, who is exiting the hall. She is described in the poem as almost seemingly made of light and that when she lifted her arms to close the door of the hall, the realm of Jotunheim became brighter. Freyr was fixated by Grid and could not take his eyes off of her. He watched as Grid made her way to her own palace and began to pay the price for sitting on Odin's sacred throne, for he longed to be by the side of the beautiful jötunn.

Freyr eventually left Odin's throne; however, he was sorrowful and did not talk to anybody. Freyr would not eat, and would simply do nothing else but think of the beautiful Grid. Freyr's father Njord was concerned for his son and could see that something was not right; thus, Njord sent Freyr's servant Skirnir to find out what was wrong with his son. Freyr told everything to Skirnir about his longing for Grid. He told Skirnir about how much he loved the beautiful jötunn and how much the other gods of the Aesir would never approve. At that moment, Freyr asked Skirnir to fetch Grid for him, regardless if his father approved of this voyage or not. For Skirnir's quest, Freyr provided his servant with his horse that was trained to travel through the most severe darkness and was fearless in the face of fire and magic. To further aid Skirnir on his venture, Freyr provided his servant with his sword that could slay even the fiercest of jötunn. He would hand over these items as payment for the dangerous quest he was sending Skirnir on, and these items were Freyr's two most prized items. In hindsight, the god of peace and prosperity would regret losing his sword when he is to face Surt in the midst of Ragnarok.

Skirnir humbly accepts Freyr's request and ventures forth on his quest to Jotunheim. Skirnir arrives at the home of Gymir, where he is faced by ferocious hounds chained at the enclosure that surrounds the jötunn's great hall. However, Skirnir continues his journey and rides towards a cowherd sitting on a mound, and he begins to ask the herder several questions. However, their conversation is being overheard, as Gymir can hear every word. Gymir is intrigued and sends over one of his slaves to invite Skirnir into his home. Skirnir enters the jötunn's home and sees that Grid is present. Grid asks what the reason is for his unannounced visit. Skirnir goes on to explain the nature of the situation and that he had been sent by Freyr to court her.

Skirnir offers a proposal to the beautiful jötunn in order to entice her to accompany him back to Asgard. Skirnir offers Grid eleven golden apples; however, Grid outlandishly refuses as she states she would never accept these apples for any mortal pleasure. Skirnir proposes another alternative and offers the ring Draupnir (the ring Odin laid on Baldur's funeral pyre), but yet again, Grid refuses, explaining that there is no lack of gold in the halls of her father's court. Skirnir is incredibly frustrated and threatens the jötunn with death and that he will decapitate her father Gymir if she refuses to accompany him back to Asgard, but this too has no effect. At his wit's end, Skirnir tries one last time and threatens to curse Grid with his magic wand Ganbantein. The thought of this terrifies Grid and she finally agrees to meet with Freyr at a secluded place called Barri for nine nights.

Skirnir, pleased with himself, returns home to Asgard to tell Freyr he was successful in his mission (Encyclopedia Mythica, 2018).

Chapter 6: The Myths of Norse Mythology

The world of Norse mythology has so many myths and fascinating tales that it is sometimes overwhelming to know where to begin. Up until this point, many of the epic tales and stories of the Norse pantheon have been discussed and highlighted. However, even so, there are so many more tales to be told; each one is as fascinating as the last. Norse mythology never fails to captivate the reader, and provide us with stories that capture our wildest imaginations. Our interest has always piqued from the whimsical tales of the Norse pantheon. There are so many myths to uncover, and so many that have withstood the test of time.

The Creation Myth of Thor's Hammer, Mjölnir

This myth tells the tale of how the most sacred symbol of Norse mythology was created: Thor's hammer, Mjölnir. The story begins one day with the god of mischief, Loki, who found himself in a particularly mischievous mood, more so than usual. Loki decided that he would cut off all of Thor's wife, Sif's, gorgeous golden hair. Thor learned of Loki's blatant disrespect and was quickly fueled with rage. In a raging temper, Thor seized the mischievous Loki and threatened to break every bone in his body. In an attempt to spare himself from unimaginable pain, Loki pleaded with Thor to allow him to go down to Svartalfheim (the realm of the dwarves) and convince the dwarves, who were master craftsmen, to fashion Sif a new head of hair. Loki tells Thor that the dwarves of Svartalfheim would fashion a new head of hair that was even more beautiful than the hair he cut off. Thor listened to Loki's plea and allowed him to venture forth to Svartalfheim on his quest (McCoy, 2012).

Loki did what he did best and convinced the dwarves to forge a new head of gorgeous blonde hair for Sif. Ivadi's (the dwarf who forged Sif's new hair) sons would also forge two other marvels for the god of mischief to present to the god of thunder. The first of these additional gifts included the Skidbladnir, which was the best ship ever created and could be folded up to a size that would allow the ship to fit in one's pocket. The second gift the dwarves presented was Gungnir (Odin's spear), which was the deadliest spear ever forged.

Loki had accomplished his task, as well as secured two very powerful gifts on top of what he had originally come for; however, Loki was overcome by an overwhelming urge to remain in the caves of Svartalfheim and revel in more recklessness. Loki decided to approach two dwarf brothers whose names were Brokkr (a metalworker) and Sindri (a spark-sprayer) and began to taunt the pair. Loki began saying to Brokkr and Sindri that they did not have the skill to forge three new creations that could parallel the might of the gifts that the sons of Ivandi managed to create. Loki was so confident that Brokkr and Sindri would never live up to the level of craftsmanship of Ivadi's sons that he even wagered his head on their lack of ability. Brokkr and Sindri were not ones to step down from a challenge and they accepted Loki's wager.

As the two dwarf brothers worked, Loki disguised himself as a bee and stung Sindri's hand. When the dwarf pulled his creation out of the burning fire, an unusual sight was seen. The dwarf pulled out a living boar with golden hair; this boar was known as Gullinbursti. He gave the dark room light and had the ability to run faster than any horse in the cosmos. Gullinbursti was said to even be fast enough to run through air and on top of the water. Thus, Sindri had created the first of three marvels that the brothers would forge for Loki.

However, the brothers were not done. Sindri laid down yet another piece of gold in the raging fire as his brother Brokkr worked on the bellows. Loki, still disguised as a bee, stung Brokkr on the neck. However, this did not phase Brokkr and the dwarf pulled out the magnificent ring, Draupnir, from the forging fire. This ring was instilled with magic and had the power that every ninth night, eight new golden rings of equal weight would fall to the beholder. Thus, the second of three magnificent marvels had been forged by the dwarves.

The brothers were on a roll. Sindri would go on and put new iron on the hearth. Sindri tells his brother Brokkr that they need to be extremely meticulous for their next creation, as a single mistake would prove far more costly than their previous two. Loki overheard the brothers speaking and believed this was a great opportunity to sabotage the dwarves' work. Thus, once again, Loki took the form of a bee, except this time, he stung Brokkr in the eyelid. The metalworker's eye was incredibly swollen and blood blocked his vision, preventing the highly talented dwarf from properly seeing what he was forging. However, that did not stop the brothers from producing a hammer of unsurpassed quality. A hammer that's power had never before been seen. The dwarves named it Mjölnir, and designed the hammer so that it would never miss its mark and would boomerang back to its owner after every throw. However, the dwarves saw one flaw with Mjölnir: the handle was too short. Sindri believed this blunder ruined the piece; however, he still viewed the finished product as acceptable. The dwarves were pleased with their astounding work and were sure in themselves about the great worth that their three treasures held. The two brothers would make their way to Asgard and claim the wages that were due to them (McCoy, 2012).

However, Loki returned to the halls of Asgard before the dwarves did, and thus presented the many gifts he had acquired from Svartalfheim to the gods. Loki would give Thor Sif's new beautiful head of hair and the almighty hammer, Mjölnir. The god of mischief would give Odin the mighty spear, Gungnir, and the ring known as Draupnir. Lastly, Loki would give Freyr the boat, Skidbladnir, and the golden-haired boar, Gullinbursti.

The Norse gods were incredibly grateful and were truly delighted with their gifts from the dwarves, especially with Mjölnir, as the gods foresaw that the mighty hammer would be extremely helpful in battling jötnar during Ragnarok. Although the gods were truly grateful to Loki for securing these gifts for them, they concluded that Loki still owed the dwarf brothers his head. The gods were a race that was true to their word, after all. When Brokkr and Sindri approached Loki with knives, Loki, being as cunning as he was, pointed out he had promised them his head, but he did not promise the dwarves his neck. The brothers, unfazed, decided that instead of taking Loki's head, they would be content with sewing Loki's mouth shut and to their forge (McCoy, 2012).

The Myth of Brunhilde

Brunhilde is a character in both German and Norse mythology, and her story has been encapsulated as a common trope among many fairytales and princess stories alike. The story of how a prince awakens a slumbering princess with a kiss. Her story is told in both the poems of Edda as well as the German epic of the 1200s. However, we shall discuss the Norse origin of the legendary princess.

According to Icelandic legend, Brunhilde was a valkyrie. This means Brunhilde was a maiden warrior to the All-Father Odin. Some consider the valkyries to be the daughters of Odin himself. However, Brunhilde was not an obedient valkyrie and was rather brutish by nature. Due to this disobedience that Brunhilde showed to Odin, she was punished, and Odin sentenced her to an eternity of everlasting sleep. Brunhilde was left to slumber in a castle surrounded by a wall of fire.

However, the hero of the story was a prince by the name of Sigurd, and according to legend, he would slay a dragon that circled around the fiery fortress and cross through the flames of the castle that imprisoned Brunhilde and finally awaken the valkyrie with a kiss.

Brunhilde, forever grateful for Sigurd's bravery, is indebted to the brave prince and falls in love with her knight in shining armor. Sigurd too falls in love with Brunhilde, and the two become engaged. However, time passes, and Sigurd continues with his duties as a prince and travels without Brunhilde. On his travels, Sigurd is given a magic potion that makes the prince forget about his love for his valkyrie lover, and thus, Sigurd goes on to marry a woman by the name of Gudrun.

However, this complicated love triangle does not stop here. Gudrun's brother Gunnar falls in love with Brunhilde at first sight and decides he wants the valkyrie to be his wife. Gunnar schemes to pursue his new love interest and persuades Sigurd, Brunhilde's former lover, to help him win over her heart. Sigurd agrees, as all his love for Brunhilde has vanished. Gunnar disguises himself as Sigurd in an attempt to win over Brunhilde's heart. The deceit works for a short period of time; however, Brunhilde would realize that she had been made a fool and was tricked by her former lover.

The valkyrie, consumed with rage, would arrange to have Sigurd murdered. The deed was done and Sigurd was killed for his deceit and utter disrespect. However, as the rage in

Brunhilde's heart began to fade, she felt overwhelmed with grief and sadness as the act of what she had done hit a nerve. Brunhilde could no longer live with herself knowing that she had been responsible for her lover's death and commits suicide by throwing herself on Sigurd's funeral pyre. In Valkyrie's mind, she could join her lover once again in death.

The Aesir vs Vanir War

Within Norse mythology, there are two major tribes of gods and goddesses. These tribes include the Aesir and the Vanir, and throughout the myths, the two tribes have had many encounters. In later myths, the Vanir and the Aesir have generally gotten along; however, in early myths, this was not the case and the two tribes were bitter enemies.

The myth of the Aesir vs Vanir war began when the Vanir goddess Freya was the foremost practitioner of the terribly powerful magic art known as seidr. Like many other practitioners of the arts of seidr, she would wander from town to town offering her talented craft for hire.

Freyr eventually ventured forth to Asgard on her travels and offered her talents to the Aesir. The gods and goddesses of Asgard were greatly intrigued with Freya's abilities, and zealously acquired her services for personal gain. However, it didn't take long before the Aesir realized that their values of obedience to law, loyalty, honor, and faithfulness were being ignored. Their values were slowly being replaced with selfish desires as they obsessively desired the Vanir goddess's magic more and more.

Soon, Freya became a scapegoat and was blamed for the Aesir's shortcomings. The gods of Asgard labeled the Vanir goddess as a 'gullveig,' which translates to gold-greed, and due to her perceived deceitfulness, the Aesir gods tried to murder her. However, Freya would not die. They tried to burn her three times, but each time she would rise up once again from the ashes (McCoy, 2012a).

Due to these attempts, the Aesir and Vanir gods became bitter enemies and the two tribes began to fear and hate one another. The tension was ripe and the bitter hostilities of each tribe erupted into full-blown war. The two sets of gods fought with two very different styles. The Aesir gods were known to engage in battle through brute force with the use of plain combat and weapons, while the Vanir gods were known to fight with magic and curses. The war between the Aesir and the Vanir raged on for many years; however, it is difficult to pin down how long the warfare actually went on. The war was long, and throughout the battle, both the Aesir and the Vanir would gain the upper hand at different periods of the war. It was a stalemate, and neither tribe seemed to have been definitively winning the war.

After many years of fighting, both tribes grew tired and decided to call a truce. Calling a truce was customary during ancient Nordic times, as well as a regular occurrence with the Vikings. Thus, the Vanir and the Aesir agreed to send over hostages to live in each other's respective realms as a sign of peace. The Vanir tribe's hostages who would go on to live in Asgard were the gods and goddesses Freya, Freyr, and Njord, while the Aesir hostages who would live in Vanaheim were Hoenir and Mimir (McCoy, 2012a).

It was believed that the Vanir hostages who lived in Asgard would live more or less in peace under the watchful eye of the Aesir; however, the same could not be said for the Asgardian hostages living in Vanaheim. According to legend, the Vanir gods began to notice that the Aesir god Hoenir was able to provide incredibly wise advice to the Vanir tribe on any problem they faced; however, he was only able to do so when he was in the presence of Mimir. The fact was that Hoenir was actually rather dim-witted and was considered a simpleton who would on many occasions be at a loss for words when he wasn't around the other Aesir hostage, Mimir, to counsel him. The Vanir gods grew tired of Hoenir's simple, slow-witted replies. After Hoenir responded to the Vanir's questions with yet another unhelpful response such as, "let others decide," the Vanir believed that they had been cheated in the hostage exchange. The Vanir were furious, as they believed that they were made a fool of by the Aesir, and as a result, they beheaded Mimir and sent the hostage's severed head back to Asgard. Odin was absolutely distraught, as he loved Mimir like a brother. Odin tried his very best to revive Mimir by chanting magic poems over the head of his dead friend, and embalmed the head in herbs. Odin managed to preserve the head of one of the wisest beings in all the cosmos, and Mimir's severed head would continue to provide the All-Father with indispensable advice in times of need.

Both the Aesir and the Vanir gods were still wary of fighting a war that in the past had been so evenly matched that they feared losing too many gods through casualties. Thus, instead of engaging in battle once again as a result of this misunderstanding, the two tribes would come together on neutral ground and spit into a cauldron. Within the cauldron lay the saliva of both the gods of the Vanir and the gods of the Aesir, and through this mixture, the wisest of all beings was created, Kvasir. The creation of Kvasir was a way of symbolizing and pledging a sustained harmony between the two tribes; however, both the Aesir and the Vanir were still not fond of each other, and tension still remained in the air for many years to come.

The Binding of Fenrir

As mentioned several times before, Fenrir is the monstrous wolf child of Loki. Fenrir posed great power and possessed a violent and brutish temperament. As such, the Aesir gods of Asgard feared the power of Fenrir. The gods would desperately look for a way to subdue the beast, as they knew the son of Loki was capable of causing great destruction in the cosmos.

When Fenrir was no more than a young pup, the Aesir gods decided to keep the beast in Asgard, however, as the monstrous wolf grew at an extraordinary rate, they realized they would need to find another solution to subdue the beast from unleashing chaos upon the cosmos. At first, they tried to bind him with incredibly powerful chains by tricking the wolf into thinking the chains were a test of Fenrir's ferocious strength. However, as powerful as these chains were, they were no match for the unimaginable might of Fenrir, and he broke them with ease. No chain in the Aesir arsenal could subdue the beast, and thus, the gods decided to venture forth to Svartalfheim to garner the assistance of the master craftsman of the dwarves.

As usual, the masterclass forging talents of the dwarves did not disappoint, and they created a set of chains that could subdue the monstrous Fenrir. The dwarven chains would be forged from the sound of a cat's footprint, a fish's breath, the beard of a woman, a mountain's roots, and even the saliva of a bird. These components in unison would create the strongest chains in all the known cosmos.

The gods once again told Fenrir that the chains were just to test his strength; however, this time, Fenrir was suspicious. Fenrir said that he would only agree to wear the chains if one of the Aesir gods was willing to put their hand in the beast's mouth as insurance. The gods were hesitant until Tyr, the god of war and justice, stepped forth and was willing to sacrifice his hand if it meant that it would chain the beast once and for all. The chains would hold Fenrir, and as he said he would, he bit off Tyr's hand. Fenrir was safely subdued until the final cataclysm of the universe known as Ragnarok (Eskify, 2017).

Asgard's Wall

The myth begins one day when a highly skilled blacksmith traveled to the gates of Asgard and offered the Aesir gods his assistance in building an impenetrable wall around the realm to protect the gods from their many enemies. The gods were intrigued with the smith's offers, and listened to him intently. The smith promised that he was capable of building this indestructible wall in only three seasons; however, there was a catch. The smith said that he would only consider building Asgard's unbreakable wall if he would be duly rewarded with the goddess Freya as his wife. The gods were angered by the smith's absurd request and turned the smith down immediately. However, Loki did what he did best and managed to convince the gods to accept the smith's terms on the condition that he completed the indestructible wall in only one season instead of three. The condition would also mean that the smith could not get anybody to help him build the wall and that he and his horses were the only ones allowed to work on his proposed project.

The smith was unphased and he accepted this deal suggested by Loki and the gods. The smith began working on forging this wall with extraordinary speed, and he even managed to get his horse to help build the wall with him. The horse was said to be able to work twice as fast as the smith could. The smith was making great haste on the wall and was close to completing it. As a result, the gods watching over his progress began to panic. The gods were famous for being true to their word, and they had promised the smith no harm, as well as offering him Freya as a wife. The gods were furious and they knew exactly who was to blame. They approached Loki and commanded him to find a way to clean up the mess that he had made. Loki quickly thought of a plan and he shapeshifted into a female horse so that he could seduce the smith's horse. Loki was successful, and the smith's horse refused to carry on working, as he was smitten with Loki. The smith did not manage to finish the wall in time without the aid of his horse, and as a punishment for his failed promise, the gods killed the smith (Eskify, 2017).

Chapter 7: Ragnarok Explained

The word Ragnarok can be translated as the 'fate of the gods.' However, in old Norse literature, the meaning of Ragnarok has been played with and is also sometimes referred to as Ragnarøkkr, which means the 'twilight of the gods.' Ragnarok was given a host of other names, such as Aldar rök, which means the 'fate of mankind' (McCoy, 2018).

In Norse mythology, Ragnarok is the cataclysmic destruction of the entire cosmos and all the nine realms in it. Not even the immense power of the Aesir gods are safe from its destruction. As history can be described as linear, so can the chronological events of Norse mythology, and Ragnorok is considered the end of the set of tales the Vikings passed down to one another for generations. In respect to the

Vikings, the time in which the prophecy of Ragnarok was to occur was an unknown and unspecified period of time in the future. Although the Vikings did not know when Ragnarok was to occur, it had profound ramifications regarding how the Norsemen lived their lives and how they understood the world around them.

How it's All Meant to Unfold

Some day in the future, whenever that may be, the world will experience an icy winter like no other winter that has come before it. This winter is known as Fimbulwinter, also known as *Fimbulvetr* in Old Norse. The icy winds will be so intense that snow shall be blown from all directions across the globe, and the warmth and presence of the sun will cease, plunging the world as we know it into a frozen wasteland, crushing the flourishing of life. Fimbulwinter is prophesied to last for the equivalent length of three normal winters, with no warmth from the other seasons in between the bitterness of the snow (McCoy, 2018).

Life will not be able to grow, and thus livestock and grain will become almost nonexistent. Due to the lack of food and other essential resources, mankind will succumb to collective desperation for food and other necessities to survive; all laws and morals shall fade away and chaos shall prevail. According to experts, Ragnarok for mankind is described as an age of swords and axes, a time where lover will slay lover, brother will murder brother, the father will kill son, and son will take the life of his father. Utter barbarism and disorder shall take over as the guiding force of mankind.

The wolves known as Skoll and Hati are wolves who have dedicated their existence to hunting down the sun and the moon since the beginning of time, and will finally catch their prey. The sun and the moon will disappear, along with the stars, leaving nothing but a pitch-black void in the heavens, similar to that of Ginnungagap. Yggdrasil, the world tree that holds the cosmos together, will crumble, and as it falls, so will all the trees and mountains (McCoy, 2018).

The chains that have imprisoned Loki's monstrous wolf son, Fenrir, will shatter and the ferocious wolf will run free, issuing terror among the cosmos. Loki's other son and Fenrir's enormous sea serpent brother, Jormungand, will rise up from the murky depths of Midgard and spill all the oceans onto the earth as the treacherous sea serpent makes his way to land.

The convulsions created from the escape of Fenrir and Jormungand will shake the Nail Ship known as Naglfar. Nagalfr is a ship made entirely out of the fingernails and toenails of every dead human on the earth. Naglfar will easily sail over the flooded earth, and it will be captained by Loki, the traitor of the Aesir, who managed to break free from his confines the Asgardians bound him to. Loki would be accompanied by an enormous crew of jötnar, as well as all the forces of destruction and chaos at his disposal. Loki would marvel at the chaos the cosmos had fallen victim to.

According to legend, Fenrir will have blazing fire bursting from his eyes and nostrils and will destroy the earth as we know it. Fenrir will sprint across every inch of the earth with his lower jaw planted in the surface and his upper jaw clenched on the top of the sky, devouring everything in his way. The very little that Fenrir doesn't destroy, the sea serpent Jormungand will. Jormungand will spit venom into the oceans, onto the remnants of the land, and poison the air to make sure that no entity could ever inhabit the earth again.

The dome of the sky will be split into pieces, and from the cracks will emerge the fire jötunn from Muspelheim led by their brutal leader, Surt. Surt will enter the scenes of destruction with his flaming sword that is believed to be even brighter than the rays of the sun and begin marching his men towards Asgard. The fire jötnar will march across the rainbow bridge, Bifrost, and as they march, the Bifrost will crumble behind them.

Heimdallr will spot Surt and his endless troops of fire jötnar marching towards the gates of Asgard, in which the gatekeeper Heimdallr will blow his horn, Gjallarhorn. Heimdallr's Gjallarhorn will be heard throughout the cosmos, signaling the end of existence is near. The All-Father Odin will hear Heimdallr's warning and will realize his fear of Ragnarok has come to fruition. Odin will anxiously seek council from the wisest of all the known entities in the cosmos: the head of Mimir (McCoy, 2018).

Once Odin has sought counsel from the head of Mimir, it is clear to him what it is he needs to do. Odin declares war and rallies all of the Aesir to go to battle, despite knowing what fate has in store for them, as they are aware from the prophecies that the Aesir will meet their demise during the cataclysmic eclipse of Ragnarok. The Aesir, warriors from Valhalla, and valkyries will arm themselves with all the firepower they can muster, even joining forces with their sworn enemies, the Vanir gods. The gods will meet their jötnar foe on a battlefield called Vigrid, also known as *Vígríðr*, which translates to the 'plain where battle surges.'

The Final Battle

The battle between the gods and the jötnar will be one of epic proportions, leading to unthinkable bloodshed and destruction. The All-Father Odin will battle the blood-thirsty wolf Fenrir. By Odin's side will be the einherjar, who were the many chosen mortal warriors Odin selected from Valhalla to aid him in battle. Many believe that these mortal warriors were kept in Valhalla for this very moment. It is said that Odin and the warriors of Valhalla fought more valiantly than any warrior has ever done so before; however, their bravery and valiant efforts will go unrewarded and prove to not be enough. Odin and the einherjar will fall in battle, as Fenrir will devour them whole. However, Odin's death would not be done in vain, as one of his sons, Vidar, witnessed his father's death and would charge at the wolf, burning in rage to avenge Odin. Vidar wore a shoe that was crafted for this very moment, as it was prophesied to the gods that this would occur. The shoe was crafted from all of the discarded leather mortals threw away. Odin's son would use this shoe to hold open the blood-soaked mouth of Fenrir and stab the beast in the throat with his sword. Vanir avenged his father and Fenrir was dead (McCoy, 2018).

However, the battle between Odin, Vidar, and Fenrir is only one of many epic battles that will commence on the battlefield of Vigrid. In another event, the Norse god of war, Tyr, will battle another ferocious wolf by the name of Garm. It is prophesied that Tyr and Garm will both end each other's lives in this battle. While that battle commences, the gatekeeper of Asgard, Heimdallr, will engage in battle with the god of mischief, Loki. Much like the battle between Tyr and Garm, both Loki and Heimdallr will kill each other. However, Heimdallr is said to have taken delight just before he died for being the one responsible for finally putting an end to the trickster Loki's treachery. While Loki may have finally been silenced after all these years, the Aesir take a heavy loss by losing one of their greatest ever warriors in Heimdallr.

The battles continued to commence, and the next battle to be highlighted is the battle between the god Freyr and the brutal leader of the fire giants, Surt. The theme of Ragnorok's epic battle remains true, and both Surt and Freyr would be responsible for ending one another's lives. The last major battle to be highlighted during the battle of Ragnorok is between Thor and his lifelong nemesis Jorgmumgand; however, there were still plenty of other battles all unfolding at once. Thor and Jormungand have waited for almost eternity to end one another's lives, and during Ragnarok, both mighty beings will have their wish granted. Thor would ultimately win the fight with his brute strength and would beat down the enormous sea serpent with vicious and deadly blows with his hammer, Mjölnir. The battle looked like it had been won, Jormungand was dead, and Thor would be seemingly unscathed. However, Jorgmumgand would cleverly smother himself in so much poisonous venom during the battle that even though Thor bested the beast, he would die from severe poisoning. Thus, once again, both foes would take each other's lives (McCoy, 2018).

No warrior would be left alive during the battle of Ragnorok, and Vigrid would be a sight of countless dead bodies in which blood would saturate the soil the bodies rested upon. Once the battle is over, the remains of the cosmos will sink into the sea and there will be nothing left but an empty void of nothingness. Creation, and everything that had occurred prior to Ragnarok, will be completely nullified, and it would be as if the cosmos were never created in the first place.

The Rebirth of the Cosmos

According to some myths, it is said that Ragnarok is not the imminent end of the cosmos, and although certain scholars and mythologists will argue that Ragnorok is the perpetual end of life as we know it, some argue that Ragnorok will birth a new world. The new world that shall commence as a result of Ragnarok will be a world that is green and beautiful and will arise out of the waters of the fallen cosmos.

As some myths believed all gods were to die in Ragnarok, other myths believed that there were a few survivors. According to these myths, the son of Odin, Vidar, and a handful of other gods shall survive the brutal battle at Vigrid such as Vali, Hodr, and Thor's sons Modi and Magni.

These few gods will survive the downfall of the cosmos and live joyously in the new world.

The gods were not the only ones to survive, as there were two mortals, a man, and a woman, by the names of Lif and Lifthrasir, who survived the disastrous effects of Ragnarok as well. The man by the name of Lif translates to 'life,' and the woman by the name of Lifthrasir translates to 'striving afterlife.' Both Lif and Lifthrasir would have managed to hide from the cataclysm in a place of safety known as Hoddmímis Holt. The surviving mortal man and woman will rise from the ashes and surface from their place of hiding to repopulate the luscious green land in which they now call their new home. A new sun will arise who will be the daughter of the previous sun that was devoured and will bring an end to Fimbulwinter. A new almighty ruler of the Aesir will take over the mantle left by Odin, and the cosmos will begin to be rebuilt again slowly but surely to its previous glory (McCoy, 2018).

The Meaning of Ragnarok to the Vikings

As mentioned before, the myth of Ragnarok has two conclusions to the epic cataclysm that is present in various Norse sources. The one conclusion hints at the destruction of the cosmos and everything in it with nothing left but an empty void with no mention of a rebirth that follows the tragic events. However, the other conclusion hints at rebirth and how the cosmos will rebuild itself and rise from the ashes.

It is believed that the conclusion where no rebirth is hinted at is the older version of the epic tale of Ragnarok and constitutes a greater pagan perspective of the cataclysm. However, the conclusion that states that rebirth is to occur is an addition to the original tale, and one that was developed later on in the Viking Age under Christian influence.

The rebirth of the cosmos after the events of Ragnarok is considered a reinterpretation of the cataclysm and describes the religious transformation the Viking world was undergoing at the time. The Vikings were beginning to be influenced by Christianity, much of which had to do with the lands in which they were pillaging and raiding. Thus, this Christian influence had an effect on the Vikings, and their pagan gods were beginning to slowly be phased out and were gradually being replaced with other beliefs. Evidence of this is based on the fact that the mentioning of the rebirth is only discussed in three very late sources of the Viking Age. One of these sources was completely dependent on the other two while every other source that speaks of the events of Ragnarok does not mention a rebirth, and rather speaks of the complete destruction of the cosmos with no chance of rekindling (McCoy, 2018).

What Ragnarok Meant in the Minds of the Vikings

The question is how did the idea that the world would eventually come to an end with no chance of rebirth affect the minds of the Vikings? Well, to fully understand this, we need to put ourselves in the shoes of a Viking during the Viking Age. Picture this, you are a Viking, and you live in a world that you have been led to believe throughout your existence will be obliterated with no chance to rekindle. The very gods in which you have believed in all your life to be incredibly powerful and all protective of you will perish, and their fate of demise has been set in stone. You as a Viking would believe that nothing will be spared, not your children, your wife, your belongings, or anything that holds value to you. Now that you understand that the thinking of the Vikings was about the inevitable fate of the cosmos, you must ask yourself how that would make you react.

How does such a fate sit with you? In the present moment, how does the world look to you, knowing that everything you know has been decided to be stripped away from you and the seeds of destruction have already been sown? In your mind, your world as you know it is coming to a final conclusion of nothingness, and there's nothing you, or even the gods you believe in wholeheartedly, can do to stop it. Fate seemed incredibly gloomy as a Viking, and as such, in their minds, it seemed incredibly difficult to escape the conclusion that Ragnarok would be the demise of everything. This is how the Vikings saw the world, and this is why the Vikings were a brutal, coldhearted, and ruthless civilization that took what they wanted when they wanted, as they believed that Ragnarok would do the same to them when the time came (McCoy, 2018).

How the Thought of Ragnarok Influenced the Vikings

Although Ragnarok weighed on every Viking's mind and brought an air of despair to the

Norsemen of Scandinavia, it is important to remember that the Vikings were warriors and some of the bravest humans in history the world has ever known. Ragnarok carried various other meanings to the Vikings, one of which completed yet altered the Norsemens' tragic view of life. Although Ragnarok served as a prophecy for the Vikings' inevitable future, it also served as a paradigmatic model for human action among the mighty Vikings.

The tale of Ragnarok may have sealed humanity's fate in the minds of the Norsemen, but it did not produce hopelessness. In fact, it often served as a means of inspiration and invigoration. The Vikings believed that just as the fate of their gods was sealed, so was humanity, and just as the gods would face their gloomy fate with honor, courage, and dignity, so too would the humans. Believing in this logic, the Vikings were fearless and were not afraid of death. They knew death was inevitable, and thus, they would go into every battle fearless, face all challenges head-on, be ready to face misfortune, and be spurred on to hold noble attitudes (McCoy, 2018).

Chapter 8: How Norse Mythology Influenced Modern Pop Culture

In the last 100 years or so, Norse mythology has made a resounding comeback and has become relevant in the minds of the world's populace once again. Much of this resurgence of the old Norse beliefs regaining popularity has to be credited to its resounding influence over various properties in pop culture. By now there isn't a single medium where Norse mythology hasn't played a part in influencing some sort of portrayal of the ancient Norse pantheon. Whether it be books, movies, TV series, video games, board games, music, or even advertisements, the Norse gods are back and they are back with a bang. Some incredibly notable franchises and pop culture properties that the Norse pantheon and Vikings have influenced include *Game of Thrones*, Marvel's comic line *Thor, The Lord of the Rings*, the video game *God of War*, the introduction of Viking metal, and many more.

Norse mythology is incredibly fascinating, and it is no wonder Hollywood, writers, and game studios have jumped on the bandwagon. The tales are epic, the battles are fierce, the drama is plentiful, and the whimsical appeal of the Norsemen and Norse pantheon sure know how to reel in a crowd. Norse mythology, especially in recent years, has been oversaturated with pop culture references and portrayals of ancient legends. Whether it be Thor, Odin, Loki, Heimdallr, Fenrir, and the nemesis of the Aesir, the jötnar, they are all fascinating and deserve the attention of the world once again. The stories and tales are here to stay, and the world cannot wait to see what pop culture has in store for the notorious Vikings and legendary Aesir.

Marvel's *Thor*

Perhaps the most relevant Norse mythological portrayal of all modern pop culture can be credited to Marvel's highly successful comic line *Thor*. It is also largely credited for the overwhelming resurgence of Norse mythology becoming a part of the public's collective consciousness once again. The god of thunder has captivated the imaginations of millions with his countless adventures across the nine realms on the panels of comic books, as well as on our movie screens. Thor has been a staple character of the Marvel universe since the 1960s, in which fans all over the world have enjoyed reading about his many adventures in Midgard, Asgard, Jotunheim, and more. The Marvel comics do not only portray the god of thunder, but pretty much all the Norse pantheon. After over 60 years of comics, we fans have been entertained by stories of Thor, Odin, Loki, Heimdallr, Frigg, Helheim, Fenrir, and many more.

There have been countless epic battles between Thor and the jötnar, Thor and his nemesis Loki, and many other tales influenced by Norse mythology. Although Marvel's depiction of the god of thunder is not a perfect portrayal of Norse mythology, it is definitely a love letter to ancient mythology. Marvel has taken some liberties with retelling the epic myths of the much-loved mythology, but it is incredibly clear the influence that these ancient tales played in inspiring this beloved comic line. However, Marvel did not stop at comics alone, and have released three extremely successful blockbuster hits, which were widely popular and well received. Thor has also played a massive role in Marvel's cinematic universe, appearing in many of their other movies, most notably the three beloved *Avengers* movies that the public adore. Marvel's extensive comics featuring Thor, and Chris Hemsworth's portrayal of Thor in the cinematic releases, has truly captured the embodiment of the Norse god of thunder and provided a generation with an appreciation for the ancient Norse gods once again.

How the Vikings and Norse Mythology Influenced J.R.R Tolkien and *The Lord of the Rings*

J.R.R Tolkien was an incredibly talented author who wrote a franchise of fantasy books that took the world by storm; those books were none other than the famed *Lord of the Rings* series. *The Lord of the Rings* franchise consisted of three books, three movies, and would be the inspiration to the spin-off franchise *The Hobbit*, which had the book and three movies. It was an insanely popular cultural phenomenon that encapsulated the imagination and interest of millions of fans. However, what most people don't know was that the Vikings and Norse mythology played a significant role in inspiring the esteemed author Tolkien into creating the franchise we all now know and love.

J.R.R Tolkien was incredibly fascinated with Scandanavian culture, and much of that had to do with his Icelandic nanny, who lived with Tolkien and his family in Oxford, England, in the early 1930s. It was through the tales that his nanny told him as a child that made the author further acquainted with Norse folk tales and the mythology attached to those very stories. Tolkien incorporated those stories into his writing, and it is evident regarding the aspects of the landscape, the language, setting, and plot aspects that helped him shape the legendary fantasy world of Middle Earth.

Due to Tolkien's fascination with Norse mythology and the culture of the Scandinavian Vikings, he began to become increasingly familiar with the texts of the Prose Edda and the Poetic Edda. The writings within the Eddas also helped inspire the famous opera *Der Ring des Nibelungen*. An all-powerful ring and a broken sword are both crucial elements of both Wagner's famous opera and Tolkien's iconic *Lord of the Rings* series, and both were inspired by the accounts in the Eddas.

As evident in the title, *The Lord of the Rings*, the ring in the novel is the crucial aspect that ties everything together, and what the story revolves around in Tolkien's novels. In Norse mythology, rings and swords were incredibly significant symbols and were prevalent throughout the poems found in both the Eddas. However, according to Norse mythology, the most powerful and magical of the rings were Odin's ring and the rings of the Niflungs (any race of dwarf who possessed a treasure, generally a ring, that would provide the wearer with unlimited power). Both Odin's ring and the rings of the Nifling were forged by dwarves just like the rings forged in *The Lord of the Rings* franchise. What is also significant to note about the rings in *The Lord of the Rings* is that nine of the twenty power rings were given to the mortals. This is noteworthy, as the number nine holds significant value in Norse mythology, as mentioned in previous chapters.

In Norse mythology, rings were used as a metaphor to symbolize power, thus the idea that the power rings of *The Lord of the Rings* were all-powerful. During the Viking age, when you owned a ring, it symbolized that you were powerful and strong, and when you would share a ring with somebody else, it meant you shared property together; thus, this tradition has become a universal sentiment in modern marriage ceremonies. What also needs to be noted is that in Norse mythology, all famous swords were named and given a back story, which is evidently similar to the swords that belonged to the main characters of *The Lord of the Rings,* such as Gandalf's sword Glamdring.

However, it is not just the element of the power ring that is heavily inspired by Norse mythology. Other aspects of Tolkien's fantastical world of Middle Earth draw similarities from Norse mythological beliefs such as the elves and dwarves who are heavily inspired by the poems of the Prose and Poetic Edda. Gandalf, who is arguably one of the most popular and powerful figures of the entire franchise, is often associated with a connection with the All-Father Odin, especially in his appearance and design. Gandalf, much like Odin, sports a long white beard, wears a wide-brimmed hat, uses a staff as his weapon of choice, and is clothed in a white cloak. If Gandalf's appearance wasn't enough to showcase Odin's influence on the character, there is also the fact that Gandalf is also often associated with spreading wisdom, truth, and knowledge throughout Middle Earth.

Tolkien even took inspiration to help shape the geography and setting of his fantasy world of Middle Earth. Not only is Middle Earth the direct translation of the mortal realm Midgard in Norse mythology, but Midgard was also known as only one of three realms that were home to mortals, dwarves, elves, and giants just like in *The Lord of the Rings'* Middle Earth. The only other two realms other than Midgard that the mortals could live in were in Valhalla (Asgard) and Helheim. However, it was not only Middle Earth that shared similarities to locations described in Norse mythology. In *The Lord of the Rings,* there is a realm known as Valinor, which is described in an incredibly similar manner to the realm of Asgard, home of the Aesir gods. *The Lord of the Ring's* Valinor is described as being home to the Valar, who are the equivalent of the gods in Tolkien's novels, and instead of being located above Middle Earth, it is located to the far west of it. Valinor's described appearance and nature of ambiance also inherits various similarities.

Thus, with all these similarities that are evident between Tolkien's novels and that of Norse mythology, it is fair to say that the esteemed author was definitely influenced by the tales his Icelandic nanny told him as a child.

Viking Metal

Norse mythology did not only play a part in influencing many books, TV series, films, and video games, but also played a role in music and birthed the musical genre known as Viking metal. Viking metal is a genre of music that is a subgenre of heavy metal. Viking metal is characterized and grounded by a lyrical focus on the Norse gods, myths, Nordic legends, Nordic pagan beliefs, and the Vikings. The genre itself is a relatively diverse one and inherits various musical styles and backgrounds; therefore, many people and music lovers consider the genre of Viking metal to be a cross-genre rather than a stand-alone genre. However, Viking metal is more often than not believed to have been born from the influences of black metal and Scandanvian folk music. There are many common traits and artistic music choices that are present in the Viking metal genre that are also found in other musical genres; these include a slow-paced and heavy-riffing style of music.

The genre was founded in Scandinavia around the late 1980s-early 1990s and has shared many opposing views of Christianity, much like that of the musical genre of black metal and other heavy metal genres. However, Viking metal is not Satanic and, in fact, rejects Satanism and occult themes, and alternatively, creates music in favor of paganism, the Norse gods, the Nordic myths, and the notorious Vikings. The lyrics, sound, and imagery used by Viking metal bands are often similar and fall in line with that of other pagan-themed metal bands, although there are slight differences between pagan sub-genres in music, especially surrounding the imagery of the Norse gods and Nordic myths. The genre of pagan metal is often associated with a broader focus on mythological influence than other pagan bands, and uses folk instruments more extensively, while Viking metal distinctly focuses only on Norse mythology/paganism as opposed to paganism as a whole (Wikipedia, 2021a).

Many scholars view Viking metal to be a genre that forms part of a modern pagan movement known as the neo-völkisch movement. This means it is a genre that is trying to renew the interest in and celebration of Vikings and Norse mythological beliefs to the greater public through a resurgence of the ancient religion through music and artistic expression.

God of War

The fourth canon installment of the much-loved video game series of *God of War* is heavily rooted in the influence of Norse mythology. The majority of the Playstation 4 exclusive release is set in Ancient Norway in the mortal realm of Midgard. The video game actually predates the Viking Age, and instead of being set during the age of the Vikings, it takes place during a time where Midgard was supposedly inhabited by mortals, jötnar, elves, and other magical creatures. Other realms that can be found in this *God of War* installment include Alfheim (home of the light and dark elves), Helheim (the icy Norse equivalent of Hell), and Jotunheim (the realm of the ferocious jötnar). These are just realms part of the main storyline of the fourth *God of War* video game. Other realms that the player has options to explore if they want include Niflheim (the icy realm and coldest region of all the cosmos) and Muspelheim (the realm of fire ruled by Surt). However, the other realms in the cosmos have been blocked off, and thus Kratos, the main protagonist, cannot enter. This is because Asgard, Vanaheim (home of the Vanir gods), and Svartalfheim (the realm of the dwarves) have been blocked off due to the wrath of the All-Father Odin (Kumar, 2020).

As Kratos, you are able to travel from each realm that is accessible to you thanks to the Bifrost, which is connected to the world tree Yggdrasil at the center of the realms that connects each realm together in the cosmos. In the game, the Bifrost is located within a temple at the center of a lake known as the Lake of Nine, in which Kratos can travel to and from realms as he pleases. According to the *God of War*, the temple was created by the god Tyr, who was a peaceful god of war. However, he was killed by the hand of Odin, as he was believed to be aiding the jötnar and was scheming to try to overthrow Odin to become the new king of the Aesir.

In *God of War* 4, Kratos comes across many iconic figures in Norse mythology on his quests, such as Loki's son, Jormungandr (also known as the Midgard sea serpent) Thor, Odin, Heimdallr, and many more. There were also many iconic boss battles in this installment that Krotos has to defeat, which include Baldur, the valkyries, many jötnar, dark elves, Magni, and Modi (Thor's sons), and Matturgr Helson (the gatekeeper of Helheim) (Sayers, 2018).

This installment of the *God of War* franchise takes further inspiration from Norse mythology, as much the game focuses on runestones and runic symbols. This is significant, as Odin was considered the god who discovered the secrets hidden within the ancient rune alphabet. A runestone was typically a raised stone that was inscribed with letters of the rune alphabet. However, the runic inscription on the stone does not necessarily have to be on a runestone, as the term can also be implied as a runic inscription on boulders and on bedrock. The tradition of inscribing messages on a runestone began in the 4th century in Scandinavia and survived way into the early 12th century. However, most runestones can be traced to the late era of the Viking era from around the 9th-11th century. Runestones are significant to the Vikings as they generally were not a literate culture, and thus, they never left the world with much of a literary legacy. However, the Vikings did have an alphabet known as the runic alphabet and would describe themselves and the world around them on stones using the alphabet they believed was gifted to them by the All-Father Odin (Kumar, 2020).

Hellblade: Senua's Sacrifice

The video game *Senua's Sacrifice* is a dark fantasy action-adventure game that was influenced by Norse and Celtic mythology. This video game installment was released in 2017 and was developed by British video game development studio Ninja Theory. The game's story follows the adventures of the female protagonist Senua, a Pict warrior that ventures forth on a quest to Helheim. Senua's mission is to rescue the soul of her dead lover from the clutches of Loki's daughter Hel, who is the goddess of Helheim. On her journey to Helheim, Senua must defeat various monsters, creatures, and otherworldly entities in order to rescue her lover from spending the rest of eternity in Helheim (Kumar, 2020).

Ragnarok

Ragnarok is a Norweigan Netflix original series grounded in the genre of fantasy drama which has been largely influenced by Norse mythological beliefs. Firstly, it is evident in the title *Ragnarok*, which is the Norse equivalent of the apocalypse, that this series was inspired by the ancient beliefs of the Vikings. There are more references by name to Norse mythology as the setting the story takes place in is known as Edda, which is in reference to the Poetic and Prose Edda.

The plot takes place in Edda, which is plagued by the ferocious effects of climate change due to the pollution that is being excreted by the surrounding factories of Edda. The large majority of these factories causing this accelerated wave of climate change are owned by the antagonist family known as the Jutul family, who is the fifth-richest family in all of Norway. The Jutuls all turn out to be jötnar who are posing as mortals.

However, the protagonist of the story is a teenage boy by the name of Magne who has just recently moved to the town of Edda with his family due to his father recently passing away. Magne recognizes the pollution in Edda and comes to the realization that the Jutul family is responsible for the accelerated climate change effects. Thus, Magne challenges the powerful jötnar family for their blatant greed and disregard of the world around them. It turns out that Magne is actually the embodiment of Thor and comes into his newfound power through puberty. Magne, armed with all the powers of Thor, begins to fight anybody who shows blatant disregard for the planet, and he has his eyes set on taking down the Jutul family of jötnar (Kumar, 2020).

It is an interesting take on Norse mythology and it is quite amusing to see how the themes of Norse mythology and modern-day issues such as climate change interconnect in a cohesive narrative together.

Game of Thrones

Game of Thrones is considered by many to be one of the greatest TV series of all time, and even in all of its glory, it was largely inspired by Norse mythological events, tales, and symbolism. However, due to the immense influence that *Game of Thrones* took from Norse mythology and the immense length and universe of *Game of Thrones* we will highlight only a few similarities and symbolisms that connect these two cultural phenomena together

From the very first episode of *Game of Thrones,* fans from all over the world would be warned that "winter is coming." This phrase would become the catchphrase of the monumental series. Since the start of the series, the White Walkers were growing in numbers on the other side of the Wall of Westeros. White Walkers were humanoid supernatural beings with frosty skin, eyes like ice, and were nearly indestructible beings. They were represented with many similar characteristics as the frost jötnar in Norse mythology (Sons of Vikings, 2019).

The White Walkers symbolized the jötnar and they were growing in numbers to attack one day to end the world, similar to that of Ragnarok. While on the other side of the wall, the living were embroiled in civil war, intrigues, and accelerated chaos, mostly unaware of the danger that would eventually unravel. This is very similar to the civil war between the Aesir gods and Vanir gods who engaged in civil war amongst one another for countless years while the jötnar army was preparing for all-out war on Asgard and the cosmos. While we as the audience do not know what is going to happen come the final season of *Game of Thrones,* it has been made very clear to us that the series was headed towards a great cataclysm that would result in the destruction of everything the world had ever known.

This all ties into Norse mythology because the Vikings believed that the world would come to an end as a result of a tremendous battle of epic proportions between the gods and the jötnar, in this case between humanity and the White Walkers. This battle would be known as Ragnarok and would occur when a brutal winter engulfs the Earth and the jötnar breach the gates of Asgard. The barrier that separates the jötnar and the Aesir is the Bifrost bridge; however, the equivalent in the *Game of Thrones* series was the wall of Westeros. To fight against the onslaught of the jötnar, Odin would source the bravest warriors in all of the cosmos and Valhalla, even if they had been enemies of the Aesir in the past, in order to fight as an impenetrable unit to defeat the jötnar during Ragnarok. Similar scenes and story arcs are present in the award-winning series *Game of Thrones* (Sons of Vikings, 2019).

In Norse mythology, jötnar could only truly be harmed by the gods. The gods would often have to rely on their sacred magic weapons (Odin's spear, Gungnir, or Thor's hammer Mjölnir) to kill the jötnar. Similarities to this can be seen in *Game of Thrones,* as the White Walkers are only susceptible to damage if they are struck down by Valerian steel or dragon glass. It is also important to note that when the White Walkers would kill somebody, their victim would be resurrected as a wight, which is a zombie-like creature. It is possible that also drew inspiration from Norse mythology, as according to the legend, the jötnar who are slain during Ragnarok will be brought back to life as an undead warrior to continue their battle due to the help of the goddess of Helheim, Hel, and her undead hordes. These are just some of the many similarities between the extremely well-received TV series *Game of Thrones* and Norse mythology (Sons of Vikings, 2019).

Conclusion

Norse mythology is a truly fascinating pagan belief system filled to the brim with exciting tales, myths, gods, goddesses, customs, traditions, and stories. Throughout our read, we have peeled back the many complex layers of history that surround the Vikings and their Nordic beliefs. We have learned so much and have truly encapsulated what life was like for a Viking, how their belief system shaped their lives, and how their many gods shaped society and everything in it. Everything we need to know about the Norse pantheon and Norse mythology has been neatly wrapped in one read that provides us with a beautiful window to view what the world was like over a thousand years ago.

We covered it all, starting with the geography of the complex structure of the cosmos in which the universe coexisted with nine realms. How these realms such as Niflheim, Muspelheim, Asgard, Midgard, Jotuneheim, Vanaheim, Alfheim, Svartalfheim, and Helheim all had their own specific geographic composition and were the allocated homes of the various characters of Norse mythology. How all these realms were connected by Yggdrasil, and how all these realms were connected to Asgard through the Bifrost. We unpacked the origin of the cosmos and how all life began with Gunningagap, a black empty void of magical power that led to the creation of the first realms made of fire and ice, Niflheim and Muspelheim. We covered that from the creation of the realms of Niflheim and Muspelheim the giants Ymir and Auðumla were created and how their existence was incredibly vital for all that was to unravel in the cosmos. Ymir gave birth to the race of jötnar and Auðumla would give birth to the first gods. The creation of the jötnar and the gods would go on to form a fierce hatred between the two races and lead to unimaginable bloodshed for years to come. We learned how the creation of the other seven realms was from the help of Odin and his brothers in defeating the evil Ymir who posed a threat to the gods and all of the cosmos. We unpacked how Odin and his brothers created mortals out of tree bark to inhabit Midgard and how the world as we know it was created by the remains of Ymir and his decaying corpse. From Ymir's death, we learned how the Asgardians ruled over the cosmos and how Odin, the All-Father, would watch over all of the nine realms from his throne in Asgard.

However, just as the creation of the universe and the gods needed to be discussed, so did the Vikings of the Viking Age and how they worshipped these very gods. The Norse gods and goddesses played a significant role in the lives of the Vikings and were responsible for shaping their society and how they lived their daily lives. The Vikings worshipped their gods and goddesses in many ways. The Vikings adopted many customs and traditions in which they would practice to honor, respect, show admiration, and attempt to secure favor from the gods. The Norse pantheon was to be respected and honored in plenty of customs and traditions, such as blot sacrifices, human sacrifices, wedding ceremonies, infant ceremonies, burial traditions, Yule celebrations, and even ward off evil spirits. The Vikings wholeheartedly believed in and worshiped the Norse pantheon and much of their life was centered around the gods and goddesses they believed were protecting them. They knew the gods were not all-powerful and had their faults, however, the Vikings placed great trust, respect, admiration, and honor to their name. The traditions, customs, and beliefs of the Vikings were collectively practiced throughout Scandinavia and were a great part of a Viking's identity and general lifestyle.

There were many gods and goddesses who were worshiped by the Vikings, most of which belonged to the tribe of gods known as the Aesir. However, there were exceptions, and sometimes gods of the Vanir tribe were also worshiped, such as Freya and Njord. More surprisingly, gods who belonged to the jötnar race like Loki would also be worshiped by the Vikings, as they lived in Asgard on occasion. There were many gods and goddesses of Norse mythology who were worshiped, including Odin, Frigg, Thor, Baldur, Heimdallr, Vanir, Tyr, Loki, and many more. All these gods and goddesses represented the human condition and played a role in the greater cosmos. These gods were extremely powerful, but not all-powerful, as they had faults and weaknesses and felt human emotions, often succumbing to them. The gods and goddesses were ever-present in the myths of Norse mythology, and were ever-present in the minds of the Vikings, thus leaving a significant legacy in history. The myths and tales of the Norse gods and goddesses were well known among the Norseman and they would be passed down from generation to generation keeping the legacy of the gods alive. The gods were ever-present in the minds of the Vikings and helped the Norseman understand the world around them.

Thus it is fair to say the Norse pantheon left an enormous legacy behind for the Norse populace of Scandinavia. Almost all of that legacy can be found in two sources, which make up the overwhelming majority of what we know in the 21st century about the Norse pantheon and the Vikings. These sources are known as the Poetic and Prose Edda. The Eddas are full of epic poems that highlight the myths and tales of the gods and provide us as historians with the much-needed insight to understand the Viking mind and what it is the pagan Vikings believed in. Poems such as the Poem of Vafþrúðnismál (Vafthundnir's Sayings), the Poem of Þrymskviða (Thrym's Poem), the Poem of Hymiskviða (The Lay of Hymir), and the Poem of Skírnismál (Skirnir's journey) all give us invaluable insight into the adventures that the Norse pantheon experienced. The poems of Edda also highlight many other interesting myths, such as the creation myth of Mjölnir, the myth of Brunhilde, the Aesir vs Vanir war, the binding of Fenrir, and the myth of the Asgard wall. These poems and myths found in the two Edda's are not simply tales meant to entertain per se, but they are also stories full of life lessons and interesting facets of the human condition. These myths give depth to the Norse pantheon and provide us with knowledge about the gods for who they are. It is important to note that in these myths the gods are not all-powerful and have their own faults and challenges they need to overcome.

However, one myth in the Eddas is truly significant and is the myth that ends all myths. This myth is known as Ragnarok, and is the cataclysmic tale of the end of the cosmos and everything in it, including the fate of demise for the gods and goddesses. It is the tale of the final battle between the gods and their greatest enemy, the jötnar, as well as the Fimbulwinter that will wipe out all of humanity. The final battle is one of epic proportions where all the Norse gods will fight with all their might, but in the end, they will not be able to escape their bloody fate. It is a truly grim tale that will leave nothing left in existence; however, it is believed in later Norse myths that Ragnarok will lead to the rebirth of the cosmos and that life as we know it will rise from the ashes once again.

As we have said before Norse mythology is truly fascinating, and as such, it is no surprise that this ancient mythology has received a resurgence in popularity in the form of pop culture. By now, there is no medium that has not been influenced by the Nordic beliefs and the Vikings, whether it be films, TV, literature, video games, or music. Some of the most famous portrayals and re-telling of the Norse myths include Marvel comics' *Thor*, *Game of Thrones*, *Lord of the Rings*, *Ragnarok*, Viking metal, the fourth canon installment of *God of War*, and *Hellblade;* however, there are many more examples. It would not be surprising to see the media flooded with more and more retellings of Norse mythology through being inspired by the epic tales the mythology of the Vikings has to offer.

If there is one thing we can take away from this book it's the immense influence the Norse pantheon played in Viking society and how the Viking age was inherently influenced by the epic tales and myths that surround this fascinating pagan belief system. What's more, is how the Vikings were truly governed by their many gods. A large part of a Viking's daily life during the

Viking Age was centered around their gods. The gods would influence their actions, thoughts, and lifestyle to a great degree. Vikings would also often honor and respect their gods as they believed the gods were always protecting and watching over them, thus they would often worship their many pagan gods to gain good favor from them and protect them from ill fate. Norse mythology is here to stay, and it is back with a bang through the legacy that these myths have stamped on modern society. Many portrayals of Norse mythology in pop culture will ensure that the Nordic belief system from over a thousand years ago will stay fresh in our minds. The Vikings may be dead, but their customs, traditions, and beliefs are as strong as ever.

References

Ancient Origins. (2019, July 16). *Frigg: Queen of Asgard, Beloved Norse Goddess, Mother*. Ancient-Origins.net; Ancient Origins. https://www.ancient-origins.net/myths-legends-europe/frigg-queen-asgard-beloved-norse-goddess-mother-009707

Ancient Pages. (2016, August 7). *Asgard: Enter The Ancient Kingdom Of The Powerful Norse Gods*. Ancient Pages. https://www.ancientpages.com/2016/08/07/asgard-enter-the-ancient-kingdom-of-the-powerful-norse-gods/

Ancient Pages. (2020, December 17). *How Did Vikings Celebrate Yule - The Winter Solstice?* Ancient Pages. https://www.ancientpages.com/2020/12/17/how-did-vikings-celebrate-yule-the-winter-solstice/

Book Rags. (2018). *Elder Edda Summary*. Www.bookrags.com. http://www.bookrags.com/studyguide-elderedda/chapanal003.html#gsc.tab=0

Britannica. (2018). Odin | Myth & History. In *Encyclopædia Britannica*. https://www.britannica.com/topic/Odin-Norse-deity

Britannica. (2019a). Edda | Icelandic literature | Britannica. In *Encyclopædia Britannica*. https://www.britannica.com/topic/Edda

Britannica. (2019b). Heimdallr | Norse mythology. In *Encyclopædia Britannica*. https://www.britannica.com/topic/Heimdallr

Britannica. (2019c). Midgard | Norse mythology | Britannica. In *Encyclopædia Britannica*. https://www.britannica.com/topic/Midgard

Britannica. (2019d). *Muspelheim | Norse mythology*. Encyclopedia Britannica. https://www.britannica.com/topic/Muspelheim

Encyclopedia Mythica. (2018). *Skírnir | Facts, Information, and Mythology*. Pantheon.org. https://pantheon.org/articles/s/skirnir.html

Eskify. (2017, January 6). *10 Epic Tales From Norse Mythology*. Eskify. http://eskify.com/10-epic-tales-from-norse-mythology/#:~:text=In%20norse%20mythology%20the%20Gods%20Odin%20and%20his

Esser, J. (2018, August 6). *10 Interesting Viking Rituals - Listverse*. Listverse. https://listverse.com/2018/08/06/10-interesting-viking-rituals/

From Baker to Edlund. (2014, December 5). *Vafthrudnir's Sayings*. Frombakertoedlund. https://frombakertoedlund.wordpress.com/2014/12/05/vafthrudnirs-sayings/

Geller, P. (2016a, October 23). *Ymir - The First Giant in Norse Mythology*. Mythology.net. https://mythology.net/norse/norse-creatures/ymir/#:~:text=Ymir%20did%20not%20marry%2C%20or%20have%20children%20in

Geller, P. (2016b, November 6). *Balder - Norse God*. Mythology.net. https://mythology.net/norse/norse-gods/balder/

Geller, Prof. (2016, November 6). *Frigg - Norse Goddess and Wife of Odin | Mythology.net*. Mythology.net.

https://mythology.net/norse/norse-gods/frigg/

Geller, Prof. (2017, January 3). *Thor - Norse God of Thunder, Lightning and Strength | Mythology.net*. Mythology.net. https://mythology.net/norse/norse-gods/thor/

Gill, N. S. (2019). *10 Important Norse Gods and Goddesses*. ThoughtCo. https://www.thoughtco.com/gods-and-goddesses-in-norse-mythology-120007

Gods and Goddesses. (2016). *Thor • Facts & Mythology about the Norse god of Lightning and Thunder*. Gods & Goddesses. https://www.gods-and-goddesses.com/norse/thor/

Gods and Goddesses. (2017). *Odin • Facts & Mythology about the Norse god of Creation and Wisdom*. Gods & Goddesses. https://www.gods-and-goddesses.com/norse/odin/#:~:text=O din%20is%20the%20Norse%20king%2 0of%20the%20Aesir%2C

Greenberg, M. (2020, November 9). *The Norse Creation Myth*. The Norse Creation Myth. https://mythologysource.com/norse-creation-myth/

Kissell, J. (2018). *Hymir's Cauldron | Interesting Thing of the Day*. Itotd.com. https://itotd.com/articles/4375/hymirs -cauldron/

Kumar, A. (2020, May 7). *How Vikings & Norse Mythology are making its way into the modern entertainment*. Medium. https://medium.com/nerdvolume/how-vikings-norse-mythology-are-making-its-way-into-the-modern-entertainment-f148c15c1d52

Learn Religions. (2016). *How Did the Norse Believe the World Was Created?* Learn Religions. https://www.learnreligions.com/creatio n-in-norse-mythology-117868

McCoy, D. (2012a). *Freya - Norse Mythology for Smart People*. Norse Mythology for Smart People. https://norse-mythology.org/gods-and-creatures/the-vanir-gods-and-goddesses/freya/

McCoy, D. (2012b). *The Creation of Thor's Hammer - Norse Mythology for Smart People*. Norse Mythology for Smart People. https://norse-mythology.org/tales/loki-and-the-dwarves/

McCoy, D. (2018). *Ragnarok*. Norse Mythology for Smart People.

https://norse-
   mythology.org/tales/ragnarok/#:~:text
   =Ragnarok%20is%20the%20cataclysmi
   c%20destruction%20of%20the%20cos
   mos

Morgan, T. (2018, November 28). *How Did
   The Vikings Honor Their Dead?*
   HISTORY.
   https://www.history.com/news/how-
   did-the-vikings-honor-their-dead

Mythopedia. (2018). *Freya*. Mythopedia.
   https://mythopedia.com/norse-
   mythology/gods/freya/

New World Encyclopedia. (2020). *Norse
   Mythology - New World Encyclopedia*.
   Www.newworldencyclopedia.org.
   https://www.newworldencyclopedia.org
   /entry/Norse_Mythology#The_beginni
   ng

Norse Mythology for Smart People. (2018).
   Alfheim. Norse Mythology for Smart
   People. https://norse-
   mythology.org/cosmology/the-nine-
   worlds/alfheim/

Sacred Texts. (2019). *The Prose Edda Index*.
   Sacred-Texts.com. https://www.sacred-
   texts.com/neu/pre/index.htm

Sayers, S. (2018). *God of War PS4 Bosses –
   The Complete List*. PlayStation

Universe. https://www.psu.com/news/god-of-war-ps4-bosses/

Skjalden. (2011, June 1). *The Nine Realms in Norse Mythology*. Nordic Culture. https://skjalden.com/nine-realms-in-norse-mythology/

Skjalden. (2020a, July 22). *Ginnungagap - The Yawning Void - Norse Mythology*. Nordic Culture. https://skjalden.com/ginnungagap/

Skjalden. (2020b, September 7). *Bifröst - The Rainbow Bridge - Norse mythology [FACTS]*. Nordic Culture. https://skjalden.com/bifrost/

Sons of Vikings. (2019, April 17). *Game of Thrones and Norse Mythology*. Sons of Vikings. https://sonsofvikings.com/blogs/news/game-of-thrones-and-norse-mythology

The Honest Modern Heathen. (2020, February 24). *Þrymskviða – The Lay of Þrym*. The Honest Modern Heathen. https://thehonestmodernheathen.com/codex-regius/in-codex-regius/the-poetic-edda/thrymskvida-the-lay-of-thrym/

Wikipedia. (2021a, March 4). *Viking metal*. Wikipedia.

https://en.wikipedia.org/wiki/Viking_metal

Wikipedia. (2021b, March 14). *Fafnir*. Wikipedia. https://en.wikipedia.org/wiki/Fafnir#:~:text=F%C3%A1fnir%20then%20killed%20Hreidmar%20to%20get%20all%20the